FORGIVING IS EASY . . . OR IS IT

FORGIVING IS EASY... OR IS IT

2nd Edition

Kathryn Seymore

Copyright © 2021 by Kathryn Seymore.

Library of Congress Control Number:		2021923690
ISBN:	Hardcover	978-1-6698-0004-0
	Softcover	978-1-6698-0003-3
	eBook	978-1-6698-0002-6

All rights reserved. No part of this book may be reproduced or transmitted in any form or by any means, electronic or mechanical, including photocopying, recording, or by any information storage and retrieval system, without permission in writing from the copyright owner.

This is a work of fiction. Names, characters, places and incidents either are the product of the author's imagination or are used fictitiously, and any resemblance to any actual persons, living or dead, events, or locales is entirely coincidental.

Any people depicted in stock imagery provided by Getty Images are models, and such images are being used for illustrative purposes only. Certain stock imagery © Getty Images.

Scripture quotations marked KJV are from the Holy Bible, King James Version (Authorized Version). First published in 1611. Quoted from the KJV Classic Reference Bible, Copyright © 1983 by The Zondervan Corporation.

Print information available on the last page.

Rev. date: 11/30/2021

To order additional copies of this book, contact:
Xlibris
844-714-8691
www.Xlibris.com
Orders@Xlibris.com
833881

Contents

Acknowledgments ix
Foreword...xi
Note from the Author...xiii

I Just Want to Be Married...1
Life More Abundantly 21
It's Not Always as it Seems...43
Jealousy: A Silent Killer...57
The Stranger Called Daddy 79
Double Whammy...89
Selah.. 111
Careful, You Might Get What You Say............................. 115
Some Things Are Worth Holding On To 139
Who Would've Known 157

This book is dedicated to my father, Jesse L. Seymore, all my children, NaTashia & James Shepherd Jr, Tiffany & Joshua Lemmons.

To my grandchildren, J.O. Jonathan, Rain, Ocean, Titus and the new one still in the oven.

To my siblings and to the memory of my mom, Alma Rogers, who has preceded us in death.

Also to my Lord and Savior Jesus name.

Acknowledgments

God is so Amazing! He has taught me and brought me a long way. I'm grateful to Him.

I thank and praise God for equipping me with the gift of vision, to write and produce works of inspiration. For showing and teaching me so much that has brought me to this point in my life. A text book couldn't do it, but life experiences did. Thank you, God for being patient with me and never giving up on me. Thank you for trusting me with the things you have. I deem them precious.

Thank you to my good friend Rhonda McCaul and Carlita Burgess for their encouraging, positive words and prayers. Rhonda and I have been friends since age 9. She knew me then and knows me now. She watched me grow through various trials and circumstances over the years. Carlita and I met through our children in Bermuda and have been friends since. Though I live in the US and she lives in the UK, we've learned the truth, that there's no distance in friendship. I appreciate you both very much.

Most of all, thank you, Jesus, for being a friend that stuck closer than a brother. Jesus was there and reminded me that he would neither leave me nor forsake me. He has helped me learn the art of true forgiveness!

Foreword

If I could sum up Kathy in one word, I would have to say *perseverance*. Kathy has that and more, such as her willingness to care and listen where most would often talk and tell you what to do first.

Jesus certainly has blessed her and is the driving force in her life. Kathy and I go way back to a time where things were much simpler. At the age of nine, living in Milwaukee, Wisconsin, we became friends and have never parted.

We faced many of the same difficulties in life as well as great things. Needless to say, I believe that if her mother, Mrs. Alma Rogers, were alive, she would be so proud of her loving daughter. In many ways, Kathy is so much like her. A dedicated mother, and friend. Plus, she stays powerful in the Lord Jesus Christ.

As you read through the pages of this book, her passion for the truth and forgiveness will shine. We all have to learn to forgive for it is not in us to do so; it is God who gives the power to forgive. Kathy has dedicated her life to him, and it shows. I love you, sister in Christ, and I always will.

Rhonda McGee-McCaul
Fredericksburg, Virginia

Kathryn Seymore is a lady I have known for many years. As a matter of fact, I have known her since she was born. As a young girl, Kathryn was creative, and who knew someone who enjoyed writing letters to friends, keeping a journal, and writing plays had the potential of becoming a published author? Kathryn did! She can allow the crafty thoughts in her head to be printed on paper in such a way that when others read them, they will be looking forward to more. This is something that over time she has mastered, and we will be able to experience this art in her writing.

I am so glad to know that Kathryn has found something that she has been gifted to share with others. I am looking forward to where her gift and abilities will take her and the world.

Your sister,
Cheryl Smith

Note from the Author

When I began this book, I was not prepared for what was in store for my life. To truly understand a thing, one should experience it first. I can now say that I understand the art of forgiveness. It starts with the decision to forgive. Then the process begins.

Over the past several years, I've been faced with many challenges, some similar to the characters in this book, that caused me to come face-to-face with the decision to forgive or not.

When we are hurt, it's a natural reaction to want to get revenge. Sometimes it seems that is the only way that we will be satisfied. When you want to please God, the best revenge is to ask the Lord to love through you. You will start out thinking about the other person but soon will realize that your heart is being molded into a heart that forgives.

I've been hurt many, many times in my life and still experience hurts. I've learned that when you are faced with a hard or difficult situation, true forgiveness is a process. The swiftness at which it occurs is to varying degrees. The rewards to forgiving others as well as ourselves are endless.

One important fact I would like to see each reader take from this book is the reality of the reward of truly forgiving.

I Just Want to Be Married

And the Lord God said, It is not good that the man should be alone; I will make him a help meet for him.
Genesis 2:18

"He's staring at you again," Gina said as she was excitedly nudging me with her elbow.

I told her to calm down and stop acting childish; after all, church service was still going on. In reality, I was just as excited as she was, but I had to be dignified and carry myself as a strong woman of God. I didn't want to appear desperate for a man. I began thinking of all my friends who had gotten married. I had been in many weddings but had never been a bride. I thought to myself, *Lord, when will it be my turn?* I felt as if I was ready. *Is this the man who would be my husband? Together, we could preach the Gospel around the world and see souls saved and set free. Is this the man who would be with me for the rest of my life? God, forgive me*, I prayed silently. It is so easy to get caught up in your own thoughts while a good sermon is being preached. *But, God, I know you understand I just want to be married.* I could feel Minister Richards watching me from time to time, and I felt like a shy schoolgirl all over again, blushing.

Just then, I heard, "Evangelist Moore, you're being called on to pray." Oh my god, I couldn't believe how easy it was to lose focus so quickly.

My pastor wanted me to come up and pray over the church. As I walked up to the altar area, I repented for getting caught up in my own selfish thinking and told God how much I love and adore him. I felt the peace of God come over me as I began to pray for the church body. The power of God began to descend, and a spirit of repentance filled the atmosphere. Souls began coming to the altar, weeping. Some stayed at their seats, weeping. People all over the church were dropping to their knees, crying out to God for forgiveness. I saw two women go over to the pastor's wife. They told her they had been gossiping about her and asked for forgiveness. Sister Rita, the pastor's wife, hugged them both and forgave them. I saw two men embracing and praying for each other. I saw a father approach his nine-year-old son. He asked forgiveness for not being a good father to him and wanted a second chance. The boy threw himself into his father's arms, and they both began to weep. I saw a deacon approach Pastor Ruffin, weeping. Pastor Ruffin just embraced him and said, "I forgive you." Some ladies even came up to me and apologized for being jealous of my spiritual gifts and admitted they had been talking about me. I felt so much compassion toward them and felt the sincerity of their hearts, and I forgave them. Things were happening all over the church.

After service was over, I was talking to Sister Rita when I heard a deep, soothing voice say, "Hello, Sister Rita, how are you?" I turned around to see Minister Richards standing there, looking finer than I had ever seen him look before. He had only been at our church four times in the past, but I noticed him. Oh yes, I had definitely noticed him. He stood six feet four inches and had caramel-colored skin, hazel-colored eyes, and a mustache with a goatee. His hair was closely cut, and beautiful black waves were throughout his hair with hints of silver. His skin was so clear; it looked like it was soft to the touch. His voice was deep and melodious. He was always well dressed and smelled good.

Sister Rita said, "Minister Richards, you remember Evangelist Moore, don't you?" As he extended his big, soft, well-manicured hand, I placed mine gently in his, and he cupped my hand with both of his.

"Oh yes, I remember Evangelist Moore. How are you, sister?" he said. Trying so hard not to blush, I said I was doing very well. Just then, Pastor Ruffin motioned for his wife to come to him, which left me standing there by myself with the most beautiful man I'd seen in quite some time. "Evangelist Moore, I was wondering if you are free to have lunch with me tomorrow at twelve thirty."

I heard myself manage to say, "I'd be honored to." After some small talk, we exchanged numbers and then said good-bye.

Before I could get out of the parking lot, Gina called me on my cell phone. "Well?" she said expectantly. I told her that Minister Richards invited me to have lunch with him the next day and that I was going. She was very happy and excited for me. She told me that she as well as others felt that the two of us made a nice-looking couple. I am a six-feet-tall woman with a slender frame.

When I woke up the next morning, I felt anxious. I kept watching the clock, waiting for eleven forty-five so I could leave to meet Minister Richards. I took particular care in every detail of my preparations because I wanted to look my best.

At lunch, we talked about everything, from childhood to church. We had a wonderful time. This lunch date led to several more and dinner dates too. We even went to the museum, the aquarium, and the zoo. People were used to seeing us together now, so we even got invited to the same places to minister. Gina was right; we did make a good-looking couple.

One day, Gina and a couple more of my friends from church came by my house. We were talking and laughing, having a good time. Just then, Becca asked me the question everyone wanted to know. "So, Evangelist Jennifer Moore, are there wedding bells in your near future?" As I looked at my friends, they were all looking at me with wide eyes. I told them that the subject hadn't come up yet.

Then Monica asked, "What's wrong with you bringing the subject up? Y'all ain't no spring chickens, Jennifer! How old are y'all anyway?" Minister Richards, now known to me as Robert, was forty-eight on his last birthday, and I would be forty-four next month. Knowing this in my head was one thing, but to actually say it sounded awful. I had never been married, and Robert was a widower for seven years with two grown children. I'd never met them, only heard of them by their father. My friends began teasing me and told me I'd better hook that good-looking man. "After all," Gina reminded me, "a good man is hard to find. So, girl, whatcha waiting for?"

After they were all gone, I was alone with my thoughts, and my thoughts were agreeing with my friends. Robert and I had been seeing each other for eleven months now. Why hadn't the subject come up? Well, I was going to bring it up to him at dinner tonight. God, help me to say the right things!

"Robert," I said at dinner, "have you ever thought about getting married again?" I was shocked at his response. His eyes rolled up into his head as if I were getting on his nerves. He took a deep breath and let it out slowly. I was even more shocked when he asked me where this conversation was going. I asked him if I had offended him by my question.

"Not really," he said. "I just think we have a good thing going and don't want to change it." Well, neither had I heard this tone in his voice, nor had I seen him so defiant before. What was going on? I felt like I was in a bad dream. I almost hated that I brought up the subject, but inside I felt I should probe deeper.

"Do you have a problem with the subject of marriage?" I asked.

"I've been there before, and it didn't end well. Now can we change the subject, Jennifer?"

"All right, Robert, we can change the subject."

Things never did get back on a smooth note that night. Robert seemed distant and distracted the rest of the evening. When he took me home, I reached for his hand and softly prayed for him. I could see heartache in his eyes. Maybe he wasn't over his wife. After all, she didn't divorce him; she died.

As I lay in bed that night, wide-awake, I spoke to God. *Lord, what is going on with Robert? Is he still in love with his wife after seven years? Why did he seem a bit bitter? Lord, I'm not even going to try to deny it. I am in love with Minister Robert Richards. If he doesn't feel the same way about me, why is he spending all this time with me? God, guide my heart and heal his in Jesus's name.* Then I drifted off to sleep.

I didn't hear from Robert the next day or the day after. I didn't know what was going on and felt betrayed and angry. I didn't do anything that should make Robert not call me for two days. He owed me an explanation, but I wanted him to come to me. I went by to see Pastor Ruffin and Sister Rita for some words of wisdom. I briefly told them of my conversation with Robert and his reaction at dinner the other night. Pastor Ruffin spoke confidently that God would give me answers and show me the way. He also encouraged me to give Robert as much space and time as he needed. They both prayed for Robert and me and told me to trust God for the truth.

The next afternoon, Robert called me and asked if he could come over to my house to talk to me. "I will be bringing Pastor Ruffin with me so we won't be alone in the house. I respect you highly, Jennifer, and I love you."

"What? Robert, now I want to know where this is going. I haven't heard from you in three days, and you call me with this! Yes, by all means, come on over. We need to get to the bottom of this *today!*" After I hung up the phone, I wondered if I was too harsh. He just caught me off guard; I wasn't expecting that. How could he say he loves me and not call me? It didn't make sense to me; I needed an explanation now.

Pastor Ruffin and Robert came by forty-five minutes later, and I ushered them into the living room. Robert sat next to me and took my hand in his and said, "I have something to tell you, and it is very hard for me." As I looked into Robert's eyes, I saw hurt, pain, and compassion. "I fell in love with you some time ago, Jennifer. Everything about you. You have brightened up my world in a way it hasn't been in so long. I could tell you were falling in love with me, and when you mentioned marriage, I panicked."

"Why?" I asked.

"Jennifer, I don't want to hurt you," he said. "And I'm sorry. My wife died of AIDS. She had a blood transfusion, and the blood was tainted. Three years ago, I tested HIV positive. I still fight with feelings of anger. I know my wife didn't pass it on to me on purpose. I fought with anger toward God because we were serving him, and I didn't understand how he could let this happen to us. Today, I went to see Pastor Ruffin, and he has encouraged me greatly. Now I realize that God is not to blame. Jennifer, I want to marry you, but I don't know what life with me would be like for you. You deserve so much better."

I was paralyzed for a few moments. I had to be dreaming. *Oh my god! What do I do, Father? We don't talk about this subject much in the church. I don't really know much about this disease. Help me, Lord. Help us!*

At that moment, Pastor Ruffin suggested that we pray. He took our hands and began to pray for us. Pastor Ruffin is such a wise man. He asked God to give us both wisdom and direct our paths and hearts. After the prayer, pastor said, "Why don't you two take some time before God, fasting and praying for his will in this? Then come back and compare revelations." After a moment of silence, Robert said that it sounded like a great idea and agreed to it. So did I.

"Robert," I said. He looked at me and reached for my hand, but I drew back. He looked horrified. "I'm sorry, Robert. Please help me to understand AIDS. I really don't know anything about it besides it can be passed on to others, but I don't know how."

Robert smiled and said, "I don't have AIDS. I have HIV. There's a difference between the two. Jennifer, will you come with me tomorrow? I want to take you to the AIDS and HIV awareness center. They can answer any questions you may have concerning the two, even how they are transmitted." I agreed.

As I lay in bed that night, sleep would not come. My mind was reeling with questions. Then it happened. Alone, in the solitude of the night, anger hit like a head-on collision. I got so angry I had to get out of bed and pace the floor. At that point, I realized I didn't know who I was angry with.

Am I angry with Robert? Why did he let me fall in love with him? Why didn't he tell me first and let me decide then instead of now? How could he put me through this? Am I angry with his wife? Why did she have to have a transfusion anyway? Then Robert would not have HIV, and we wouldn't be going through any of this. Or was it God? After all, God knows my heart and how much I love him and will do whatever he tells me to do. Somehow, it doesn't seem fair for me to have to be going through this. Why is God letting my life go crazy? I'm dedicated to him. I finally found a wonderful man who is committed to God with all his heart, loves me, and wants to marry me, but he has HIV. Wow! Thanks, God, you really do love me, huh? Hey, wait a minute. Maybe I am mad at myself. Maybe God did tell me, but I could have had my head so far in the clouds that I didn't hear him. Then again Sister Rita introduced us. It's her fault. Why didn't she just mind her own business? I wish I could go back to that day after church when she introduced me to Robert. I would have said hello and just walked away.

At that moment, I caught a glimpse of my reflection in the mirror because of the moonlight shining through my window. I turned on the lamp and took another look at my reflection. Somehow, seeing myself brought me back to reality, and what was real was that I loved Robert. His wife couldn't control her need for a transfusion. Sister Rita did nothing wrong. I love and trust God. More importantly, Robert has HIV, and I was acting like I was the victim. The truth is I can just walk away if I want to and leave all this behind and let it only be a memory, but Robert can't. He has to live with his diagnosis every day. The question is, do I want to share all that with him? So many questions, but what are the answers? I decided to try to go to sleep and deal with it all later. I turned off the lamp. Then I noticed the golden hues of the sunrise now replacing the moonlight that once filled my bedroom. What time was it anyway? I looked at the clock, and to my surprise, it was 6:45 a.m.

"Oh my god!" I said out loud. I had been up all night. Literally! At that moment, my phone rang.

"Good morning," I said, answering the phone. "Good morning, beautiful," was the response in the most soothing voice.

"Hi, Robert," I said with a blush.

"I hope I can still make you blush like that in ten years," Robert said.

"What makes you think that I'll be—never mind," I said, wishing I would have thought before I spoke.

"What were you about to say, Jennifer?"

"I don't know, Robert, I feel so confused."

"I understand, Jen. I hope this is not too early for me to be calling. I couldn't sleep at all last night, so I wanted to call you this morning to ask you when you want to go on a fast and seek God."

Wow, I couldn't believe he was up all night too. "Why couldn't you sleep, Robert?" Then there was silence on the line. "H-h-hello?" I said.

"I'm here," Robert said. "I kept seeing your face every time I closed my eyes, and I could see the pain and hurt you were feeling. Just knowing that I was responsible for it hurt me. I have been talking to our Heavenly Father all night and reading the word. I know God has something to show us, and we need to seek him to see it. I wish I could change things, Jen, but I can't. The last thing I ever wanted to do was hurt you. I didn't think I could love like this again. If it were possible, I think I love you more than I have loved anyone."

Wow, I didn't need this at this time. It was hard enough without him saying that. But I knew he was telling the truth. I couldn't just walk away because he held my heart. I couldn't go heartless. So I told him I would be ready to begin in a few days. First, I needed some time to digest things and think. I asked him, "Are you still taking me to that . . . um . . . center place to learn more about . . . um . . . you know?"

He chuckled and said, "Yeah, I'm still taking you to that '. . . um . . . center place to learn more about . . . um . . . you know.' I'll pick you up at one, okay?"

"I'll be ready, Robert. See you later." I felt so ashamed that I couldn't even say HIV or AIDS.

At the center, I felt awkward and out of place. I guess the receptionist could tell because she assured me that everything was fine. Robert had already set this meeting up with the administrator who was a very warm and friendly woman in her fifties. Her smile brought peace to my heart. After the introductions, we got right to the business at hand. She told me to ask her anything, and she would do her best to answer my questions.

"What is the difference between HIV and AIDS?" I just blurted that out.

She smiled and told me that *HIV* stands for human immunodeficiency virus and is the virus that attacks and breaks down our body's immune system. In other words, our immune system is the "internal defense force" that fights off infections and diseases. When our immune system becomes weak, we lose this protection against all illnesses and could develop serious, often life-threatening infections and cancers. Because our immune system is broken down, something as simple as a common cold can become a serious illness.

AIDS stands for acquired immunodeficiency syndrome. It is the name for the condition that people with HIV have if they develop one of these serious infections or if their immune system has been very badly damaged by the virus. It usually takes many years before HIV breaks down a person's immune system and causes AIDS. Most people have few, if any, symptoms for several years after they are infected. Once HIV gets into the body, it can do serious damage to it. People who appear perfectly healthy may have the virus without knowing it and pass it on to others.

Naturally, my next question was "How do you get the disease?" I learned that you cannot get HIV or AIDS through casual contact, such as hugging, kissing, shaking hands, or being near a person with the disease. It is spread through sexual contact (semen and vaginal fluids) and sharing syringes or from syringes tainted with blood. It is also spread from an infected pregnant woman to her unborn child. This is why many children die from AIDS. I also learned that a person could live a normal life, taking particular precautions. I was so overwhelmed with the knowledge I had acquired. I never realized that there was so much suffering going on. What an eye-opener. I thanked God for this new knowledge. I know he will use it for his glory somehow.

As we drove home, Robert broke the silence by asking if I wanted to stop and get something to eat. All I could say was "How can you think of eating after all that?"

He looked at me in bewilderment. "I'm sorry, Jennifer. I must realize this is all new to you. I've been living with it for so long now, it's just a way of life for me. Take your time with the information given you today and let God lead you. Okay?"

"Thank you, Robert. I need the time to think and pray. This is life altering," I said.

"I know it is, sweetie. Just take your time, as much as you need. You let me know when you are ready to seek God, and we will . . . together," Robert said.

"Thank you, Robert," I said softly.

Over the next few days, I spent much time in prayer for Robert and all the people with HIV and AIDS. I even went back to the center to learn more. My face became so familiar there that they began calling me by my first name. I met people with HIV and some with AIDS and became their major supporter. I often embraced and prayed for them. We laughed together and cried together. Soon I became so well-informed about these diseases that I asked Pastor Ruffin if I could teach an HIV and AIDS awareness class at church. I wanted to invite other churches as well as the community. He thought that it was a wonderful idea and asked Minister Richards to consider joining me in this quest. This was a lot to ask him, of course, so the pastor told him to pray about it and let him know. Robert was amazed at my enthusiasm to learn. This was all beyond me. It felt as if this was part of my purpose in life now. Wow, this time last month I knew nothing about these diseases and didn't really think about them at all. What difference knowledge can make. I felt compelled to inform others, especially those in the church communities. The world should be able to come to a well-informed body of Christ to get help and answers.

I was now ready to fast and seek God with Robert as the pastor suggested. We fasted three days and spoke only on the phone. We did not see each other at all during that time. When the fast was over, we met at the Mocha Shop for a hot cup of tea and to share with each other.

"Jennifer, this fast has been so refreshing for me, so much so that I feel like I've been cleansed internally."

"I know what you mean, Robert. I feel the same way."

Robert reached across the table for my hand and said, "God has completed me, and I am now a whole person. I know beyond a doubt that I am ready to share my life with you. Where do you stand, Jennifer?"

"Well," I said as I shifted in my chair, "I have complete peace with God, Robert, to share my life with you. I've learned so much from my new friends at the center, and I have a drive to teach the whole world, especially the young people, about HIV and AIDS. The youth are casually engaging in sex and are contracting HIV and spreading it without even knowing. I really can see why God intended for husbands to have sex only with their wives and vice versa. So many young people are having multiple partners and one-night stands. Abstinence is the best defense against these diseases."

At that moment, Robert pulled out a little black box and flipped it open, and there before my eyes was the most beautiful diamond ring. He knelt on one knee right there on the floor of the Mocha Shop and asked me to marry him. I was so happy and excited that my vision became blurred because of tears of joy.

Robert said, "Evangelist Jennifer Rose Moore, will you do me the honor of becoming my wife for the rest of our lives?"

All of a sudden, I became so hot that my hands began to sweat; and with one blink of the eyes, the tears fell. "Yes, Minister Robert Melvin Richards, I will become your wife."

He then placed the ring on my finger, kissed the back of my hand, and told me that he loved me. I threw my arms around his neck and embraced him.

"Jennifer, I want you to meet my son and daughter tomorrow. They both are coming over to meet you." Okay was all I could muster up to say.

The next evening, I went to Robert's house to have dinner with him and his children. I knocked on the door, and a young man answered, who looked a bit like Robert but more like his mother. As he extended his hand to shake mine, he said, "You must be Evangelist Moore. I'm Melvin, Robert's son. It's good to finally meet you. Dad has told us so much about you." I shook his hand and told him how good it was to finally meet him too. He ushered me into the kitchen where Robert and his daughter were putting on the last touches to the night's meal.

"Hi, sweetie," Robert said with a kiss on the cheek. "You met my son, Melvin. This is my baby, Valerie. Valerie, this is Evangelist Moore."

"Please call me Jennifer," I said. Melvin said that it sounded disrespectful and wanted to know if they could call me Evangelist Moore until they became better acquainted with me. "Sure," I said.

We sat and had dinner and talked all the way through. I felt as if I'd known his children for a long time. They made it so much easier because they brought me in on every conversation, making me laugh and telling on their father. We had a wonderful time. By the end of the evening, I was no longer Evangelist Moore, but Jennifer.

After dinner, Valerie and I cleared the table and went to put the dishes in the dishwasher. While we were in the kitchen, Melvin came in and asked us to join him in the family room. As we entered the family room, there was a portrait on the wall of the two of them with their mother and father. Melvin invited me to be seated first, then Valerie, and then himself.

"We asked you here without our father because we wanted to speak to you one-on-one," Melvin said.

Then Valerie spoke. "My daddy is my heart. He is a wonderful man and deserves to be happy again. He told us that you know about the HIV."

"Yes, I do," I said.

"You're okay with that?" Melvin asked.

"Yes, I am. I've learned extensively about the illness and how to live with it. I love your father with all my heart, and I want to share the rest of my life with him. Together, we can conquer anything through God."

Valerie smiled and said, "Jennifer, I've never seen my father this happy since my mother passed away. They had a beautiful marriage and served God together. They taught us that God is first in life, then your mate. Do you feel that way?"

"Yes, I do. God will always have first place in my heart, then your father."

"Good. I like you, Jennifer, and I can tell my father is crazy about you. I want you to know, if you need help in any way with the HIV, I'll be here for you. We had to learn so much when Mom was sick. We've never contracted HIV, and we all lived together, so if I can be of any help, just let me know."

"Thank you, Valerie, that means so much to me."

Just then, Melvin said, "My dad is a special man. He was my hero when I was a kid, and he still is. We are a close family. What affects one affects us all. So his happiness means so much to me. When my mother died, I watched my father wither and almost give up. Val and I prayed so much for him. Then he began to come around. He is a great man with a great heart. I can tell he loves you, and I can tell you love him too. I haven't seen my daddy this happy since before Mom died. I'm glad God brought the two of you together. What we're telling you, Jennifer, is that we approve of your union with our father. Even though I live two hours away, I'm only a phone call away. Call whenever you need to. You're welcome to visit anytime. Dad comes to see me every other weekend, and I'm here on the other weekends."

"Thanks, Melvin. You have a beautiful relationship with your father. I admire that. I appreciate you two taking the time to welcome me into your family. This is such a special moment for me. I have no siblings, thus no nieces or nephews. Holidays are pretty quiet for me. My family is really my church family. My parents are missionaries in India, so I don't see them often. When God does a work, he does it completely." I hugged them both, and we joined Robert in the living room.

He was standing near the fireplace, looking handsome. "So you survived my children, huh? I hope they were nice."

"Aw, Dad, come on now. How else would we be? You make us sound like villains," Valerie said as she went over and hugged her father. Robert laughed.

"You have wonderful children. You and Margaret did a wonderful job raising them," I said. At that moment, Robert turned in my direction and looked at me with wide eyes. "What?" I said.

His eyes softened as he said, "Have I told you lately that I love you? Have I told you there is no one else but you? You've taken away my sadness and given me gladness. You ease my trouble, that's what you do." As he walked over to me, he continued, "I'm not sure I got all those words right to that song, but that's what you've done for me." He then gently embraced me in front of his children, and they said out loud, "Awwwwwww." We all began to laugh and continued our wonderful evening together.

Sunday at church, Pastor Ruffin said to the congregation with a smile on his face that Minister Richards had something he would like to say to the church. Everyone began oohing and aahing. Robert announced to the church that he asked me to marry him and that I said yes. Gina jumped to her feet first and said, "Yesssss!" Everyone started laughing. Pastor Ruffin followed up by announcing that all this was done with his blessing. Robert and I were married six months later.

It has been five years now, and I love him more today than I did the day we married. We do extensive traveling around the world, preaching, and teaching. We teach a lot about HIV and AIDS awareness. I am HIV-free and have a wonderful relationship with my husband in every way. Once a year, we have a conference, educating and bringing revelation on the subject. Many people have claimed healing and deliverance from HIV, fornication, cigarettes, drugs, and alcohol at these conferences. We have even seen mothers infected with HIV deliver their babies without them contracting the disease. God is so powerful. This past Sunday at church, I heard Pastor Ruffin call, "Evangelist Richards, please come up and pray for the church."

As I walked to the pulpit, I could feel the presence of God engulf me. I opened my mouth to pray, and to my surprise, a song came out—one I'd never heard before. I sang about the love of God, and as I did, tears began to stream down my face. All over the church, people began to weep. Some began to lay prostrate on the floor, some knelt at their seats, and others stood with arms extended upward, with heads lifted as tears rolled down their faces. No music was playing; just the song was being sung. Then I was finished. No more would come out of my mouth. All that could be heard was weeping, wailing, and shoutings of "I love you, Lord."

I could no longer stand; my legs felt weak in his presence. I buckled and knelt in the Father's presence. All of a sudden, I heard my husband sobbing and saying through his sobs, "Yes, Lord!" over and over. I looked over to where he was sitting and didn't see him. He had gone to the altar and was lying on the floor. When things calmed down, Pastor Ruffin couldn't even preach, so he announced, "You are dismissed. You may leave if you can." Some left, but many stayed because they were in God's presence.

Two hours after we were dismissed, my husband was able to get off the floor. An usher helped him to his feet. I looked at him, and he was glowing. His face was bright, and his hair was shining. He looked ten years younger. I knew something happened while he was on that floor. As I began walking over to him, I noticed people staring at him. I guess they saw what I saw. Robert reached out to hug me, and when he did, I felt a jolt go through my body that knocked me to the floor. As I lay there, I couldn't move. I heard in my spirit these words: *I am pleased with you, Jennifer. You are an obedient daughter. This day, your reward is with you.*

The next day, I prepared breakfast for Robert and me. He ate and took his medication. A short time later, he ran to the bathroom, throwing up.

"Are you all right?" I asked.

"That never happened before," Robert said. "I felt so sick." I reached over to put my hands on him and began to pray over his body. The next morning, the same thing happened. I decided to call the doctor so we could find out what was going on. He told us to come in right away.

While we were there, they ran tests. After we had been there for a while waiting for results, the doctor came in to see us with a puzzled look on his face.

"I'm sorry, Robert, to have to put you through all those needle pricks, but we needed to do a series of tests. Now I don't know quite what to make of this, but your blood work is showing no signs of the HIV virus. That is why we took so much blood. We ran the test three times. Would you please come back Friday so we can run another to verify? I've never seen anything like this before in my life." Robert was absolutely quiet.

"Honey, did you hear what the doctor said?" Yes was all Robert could say.

As I drove home, I looked over at Robert. He was still absolutely silent. I felt that I should say nothing, so I didn't. Once home, Robert went into our prayer room and asked me not to disturb him. "Okay, baby," I said. He was in there for hours. At one point, I was tempted to knock on the door but felt as if the Lord was telling me not to. I had dinner alone, cleaned up, and went to bed.

At ten fifteen, I heard Robert open the door. He came into the bedroom. I dropped the book I was reading in bed and said, "Baby, you're glowing!" I looked at his face, and he was glowing again.

He smiled and said, "I'm going to take a shower. I'll be right back."

After he showered, he came in and got into bed. I curled up next to him and put my head on his chest. We lay there in silence for a few minutes, and then Robert said, "Sweetie, God healed my body Sunday at church. The reason I keep throwing up in the morning is because I'm putting that strong medicine into my healthy body. God said my body would reject it each time I take it. He also said for me to go back to the doctor Friday so they can verify that I am healed completely."

I rose up and looked at my husband, who was still glowing, and began to cry and praise God all at the same time. While doing so, I remembered what God spoke in my spirit on Sunday when Robert touched me and I fell to the floor: *I am pleased with you, Jennifer. You are an obedient daughter. This day, your reward is with you.* I told Robert, and we both got out of bed and began rejoicing and praising God.

After that, we were intimate, and Robert said to me as he held me in his arms, "I remember the day we officially met. God moved in that service in such a powerful way. People were repenting and asking for forgiveness all over the church. Do you remember that?"

"Yes, that was an awesome move of God," I said.

"I was just thinking how that was the start of a mighty revival in my life and others."

"How so for you?" I asked.

"Baby, that was the day you came into my life, and since then, I have grown, been challenged to grow, and desired to grow even more. Jen, you motivate me. I thank God for you every day. My soul has been revived, and now there is a stirring to challenge others. Tonight, when I was in the prayer room, God spoke to my spirit. He told me to lay hands on the sick as he leads and they will recover. Baby, there is much for us to do for his glory. I want you always by my side." I looked into Robert's eyes and loved him more than ever, but I could not say anything. I guess I didn't need to because he smiled and said, "Yeah, baby, me too."

Life More Abundantly

The thief cometh not, but for to steal, and to kill, and to destroy:
I am come that they might have life, and that
they might have it more abundantly.
John 10:10

"Carmen, I had a great time with you today. It reminded me of how we used to hang out before you got married," Anita said. She looked over at me, sitting in the passenger side of her Chevy Tahoe. "What's wrong, chica? You look sad," Anita asked with concern in her voice.

"I'm fine, Anita. I was just thinking. Spending the day with you has been so much fun for me too. I haven't laughed so much in a long time. I just hate that it has to end."

It had been so long since I had spent a Saturday with my friend. We took our time as we went shopping at Greenbrier Mall and Westgate Mall. We went to the movies to see a comedy for a good laugh and then went to Paris on the Green, the quaint outdoor French restaurant I had always wanted to go to. I felt like I did in earlier years when Anita and I did this all the time. How did my life get so far offtrack? Anita told me that she knew something was wrong and that she didn't trust Hector, my husband.

"Girl, that man has you all hemmed up in that house like it is some sort of prison. I know he doesn't like me, and I don't care because I don't like him either. I don't know why you married him anyway."

As usual, Anita was right. Something was wrong, terribly wrong, but I couldn't tell her. Since childhood, Anita couldn't hold water. She is a great person but loves juicy gossip. I knew telling her would be like going to the newspaper taking out an ad. Even when she tries not to tell something, it always seems to slip out.

"I'm not going to get in that conversation with you, Anita. Come on, it's been a wonderful day. I don't want to spoil it by talking about that. Okay?"

"Okay, chica," Anita said.

As we pulled in my driveway, my heart began to feel heavy, but I kept a smile on my face for Anita and said, "I had a great time, chica. I hope we can do it again soon."

We embraced and said goodbye. I slowly walked to the back door where Hector was to greet me with a kiss.

"Hey, Carmen, baby, did you have a good time with Anita? I really wanted you to have fun. Tell me all about your day."

I looked at Hector and said, "You know all about my day because you were constantly calling me on my cell phone, asking me where we were. You know all the places we went to and the times we got there. There's really nothing else to tell you."

Hector came over to me and put his arm around my waist and said he was glad I had fun and then kissed my forehead. "Let's go to bed, honey," Hector said. "We have to go to church in the morning."

The next morning, I got up and prepared breakfast for Hector and the boys. Then I woke them up so we could all eat. On Sunday mornings, we ate breakfast together as a family. This was something Hector insisted on. He believed that Sundays were for God and family. At least he felt that way until his friends came by in the afternoons or evenings after church.

After breakfast, I got the boys ready. Hector Jr. was five and proudly dressed himself, while I got the twins Julio and Juan, who were three, dressed. After they were ready, I got dressed. As I was putting on my clothes, Hector commented on my body. "You always were built like a man, but now that you've lost weight, you look even more like a man. Why did you lose weight anyway? You were already small."

That comment should have hurt my feelings, but I was so used to it. I just shrugged it off by saying that I was not trying to lose weight. "I can't help it. I don't have much of an appetite anymore, Hector."

"Why?" Hector asked. I told him I felt sad most of the time, and when that happens, I forget to eat. "That's stupid, Carmen. How can you be so sad with all the things that we have. I gave you this nice house and nice furniture. I bought you a nice car, and I also gave you the best kids in the world. So you see, Carmen, the problem is with you. You need help, girl. You should show some appreciation." To avoid an argument I could feel was about to happen, I just told him that he was right and that I was sorry.

Church was my time. I got lost in the singing and preaching. I always looked forward to going to church and hated to leave. As Pastor Hernandez began to preach his message, I was shocked because it was as if he were talking directly to me. When he was finished, his wife, Sister Hernandez, began to sing the song "I Surrender All." As I listened, tears began to stream down my face. The words were saying what I wanted to do but didn't have the strength or faith to do it. After the song was over, Pastor Hernandez asked for those needing prayer to come forward. I went up. Pastor came to me and leaned to my ear and asked what I needed prayer for. I told him that Hector and I were having serious problems in our marriage and that I was tired of it all. Pastor Hernandez began to pray for me and my family. As he did, I couldn't control my tears or emotion. I began to weep from the depths of my heart. Somehow, this was refreshing to me. The more I cried, the better I felt. I guess I had been holding so much in, and now was my opportunity to release them.

Sister Hernandez came to me and hugged me. As she did, I felt so safe and secure. She was a short, stout woman with humongous breasts that felt like pillows as she embraced me. I completely relaxed in her embrace. It felt like one of those motherly hugs. At that moment, I had forgotten all the problems in my life. All I could feel were peace and safety. I didn't want to let Sister Hernandez go.

When church was over, I looked over to Pastor Hernandez, and he motioned for me to come to him. He offered for Hector and me to come in for some counseling. I said, "Noooooo, Pastor! Hector must never know I said anything about our marriage. He would get so upset. Pleeeease don't say anything to him about counseling."

Pastor looked at me, bewildered. He saw horror and fear in my face. He reached out and took my hand and said, "Carmen, Carmen, it's okay! I won't say anything to Hector. I will talk to God about all this. I know there's something you're not telling me, but God knows. Don't worry, God has all this. Carmen, you just need to surrender everything to him, including yourself. Think about it, and in the meantime, remember all of us have sinned and fallen short of God's glory. God gave his only begotten son, Jesus, to die on the cross so that whoever believes in him shall never die but have eternal life with him in glory. Carmen, Jesus came to this world so that we would have life, and not just any old life, but an abundant life through him. He wants you to enjoy a joyous, productive life. He has all that for you. Think about it, okay?" Then he wrote down the scriptures John 3:16, John 10:10, and Romans 3:23 to back up what he was saying and told me to read them later.

As I was thanking him, Hector walked up to us and then put his arm around my waist and said, "Hello, Pastor. That was a good sermon. Isn't my wife a beautiful woman?" Pastor Hernandez told Hector how much he appreciated the compliment, but it belonged to God. He also told him that he had a nice singing voice and that they could use a tenor in the choir. Hector blushed and said, "Awww, thank you, Pastor, I'll think about it." Hector loved it when the attention was on him, so that was smart of Pastor to shift the conversation to him.

As we were heading to the car, one of Hector's friends shouted to him, "Hey, Hector, come here!" Hector told me to go to the car with the boys and he would be right back. As the boys and I waited in the car, my thoughts were on the service. I was thinking about the song Sister Hernandez sang and then how Pastor told me I needed to surrender everything to God, including myself. It was as if he knew my thoughts. That was what I wanted to do, but I didn't know how. It sounded so simple yet so hard. At that moment, Hector came back. "I'm going over to Caesar's house after dinner for a few hours to watch the game." I knew what that meant. He would probably come home drunk tonight. Oh well, at least the boys and I would have a quiet evening.

Once we were home, I went in to change the twins' clothes and then changed my own and started dinner. Hector was unusually quiet. While the food was cooking, I decided to do some ironing. The boys were in the backyard, playing. As I was hanging up one of the shirts I had ironed, I heard, *Whack!* At the same time, I felt that all too familiar sting of Hector's hand on the side of my face. Before I knew it, I was on the floor, with him standing over me. He yelled at me, "I know you told that pastor something about me, you—! You need to learn to keep your mouth shut." Another blow to my head made my nose bleed. "I know you like him anyway. I saw him whispering in your ear. I know you like the feel of another man being so close to you. Carmen, you—!" He kicked me in the stomach twice and then grabbed my hair. He pulled my hair so hard it felt like it came out. I begged him to stop. He said, "You're so ugly, nobody wants you! Your own sons don't even love you. You are mine, Carmen! Do you hear me? You're mine!" I was so weak and barely moving when he left the room. I began to drag myself across the floor to the corner, and I think I passed out. Then I heard Hector say, "You are my wife, my property. I'll fix you." I tried to move quickly to get away from him, but I was in so much pain. Just then, he sat on me and grabbed my left leg, and I felt a sting to my thigh. It went from stinging to burning. It was excruciating. I tried to fight him off me, but I was too weak. "There now you are branded with my iron. My iron, my wife, my property!" Hector had laid the hot iron on my thigh and burned me severely. I passed out for sure then. When I woke up, I was still lying on the floor, and I heard the boys crying and banging on the sliding glass door, which Hector had locked to keep them from coming in to see what he was doing to me.

My head felt like it weighed a ton. I felt like I had to throw up from the pain in my stomach. And my leg, that was a different story. Because the burn was so bad, I couldn't walk. I made my way to the sliding door and unlocked it to let my sobbing sons in. They all grabbed me and hugged me tightly. It was painful and soothing at the same time. My heart ached for my sons who didn't understand what was going on. Juan placed his little hands on my face and said through his tears, "Mommy, Jesus will make it all better."

Suddenly, Hector came in the front door. He made the boys go upstairs to Hector Jr.'s room. I made my way to the bathroom to try to do something for my throbbing leg. Hector came in the bathroom and told me that his sister was there and going to look after the boys while he took me to the hospital to get my leg checked. As he was helping me to the car, his sister, Bonita, said, "You'd better stop treating your wife like that before she leaves you one day."

"Shut your face, Bonita. You don't know what you are talking about!"

On the way to the hospital, Hector told me what to say if they asked me what happened. He assured me that it was all my fault and that I just needed to learn to obey him. "Stay out of that preacher's face, Carmen. I'm just trying to protect my family." Somehow, that didn't make any sense to me. If this was his protection, I didn't want it. I was silent on the way to the hospital. While at the hospital, they decided to keep me overnight. Hector didn't like that and tried to talk them out of it, but the doctor said that the burn looked like it might need a skin graft. Hector asked what that meant, so the doctor explained it to him. When we were alone in the room, Hector told me he didn't want me to get the skin graft because he wanted me to be reminded by the *brand* he put on my leg that I belonged to him. He told me to refuse it, or he would do it again. I was so scared of him at this point, so I did as he told me.

When Hector left the hospital, a woman came in to see me and told me her name was Pamela Brooks. She told me to call her Pam. She was a social worker and asked if she could talk to me. I said yes because she had such a kind face and a gentle voice. She looked to be in her thirties. She told me that she knew that my husband beat me up. I looked at her in bewilderment. "How?" I asked.

"I see women with some of the same injuries and even more. I've even seen women dead at the hand of their abusive husbands or boyfriends. The husbands always apologize later but makes sure the wife knows it's all her fault. You'd be surprised to find out how many other women in this city are suffering in the same manner as you. Do you have children?" Pam asked.

"Yes, three boys."

Then she looked a bit sad. "I hope your boys don't turn out to be like their father. Some of the cases I've worked with, the men stated that they grew up in homes where they saw or heard their fathers abuse their mothers or girlfriends." Pam told me of some horrible statistics and showed me pictures of abused women and a couple of women who had died from their injuries. The most surprising part about it all was that these families were from all walks of life, from poor to extremely wealthy. Some were churchgoers; most were not. She reached in her bag to get her business card to give me, and I saw a Bible.

"Do you read that?" I asked.

She saw I was referring to the Bible and said, "Every day!" I asked her what reading the Bible does for her. She told me that she encounters a lot of sadness in her line of work and the Bible keeps her focused on what's real and true. She said it brings her back to the love of God and helps her to love these families unconditionally.

I looked at her and said, "Even the men?"

"Yes, even the men, Carmen. Abuse is wrong, and I try to get these families the help they need. I don't make decisions for my clients. I just help them based on their rights. However, I don't advise them to stay in abusive lifestyles. Can I come back tomorrow to see you?" I told her I was only supposed to be there overnight. She gave me her business card and told me I could call her anytime.

The next day, the doctor came in to talk to me about my leg and tried to talk me into having the skin graft. But unfortunately, I was so afraid of Hector, I refused. So he told me how to treat my leg at home, and the nurse bandaged it up and told me to keep it elevated and to stay off it for a few days.

Bonita came to the hospital to pick me up. As we were driving home, she said, "Carmen, don't get mad at me for what I am about to say, but how can you stay with my brother? He treats you so bad. If he really loved you, he'd protect you, not beat you. I know he is my brother, and I love him, but he needs help! You know I am right. Papi used to hit my mommy and talk mean to her. He was nice to us and would take Hector with him from time to time. Hector said Papi had a lot of girlfriends. I couldn't wait to move out of the house. I wanted to take Mommy with me to rescue her, but she kept saying Papi didn't mean it, and she stayed there with him. Carmen, you see my mother today, don't you?"

This was a real eye-opener because my mother-in-law looked like she weighed ninety pounds wet. She used to weigh 125 pounds in her earlier years. The stress of her lifestyle with Pablo, her husband, and the lack of love showed in her worn face and body. She looked to be eighty, but she was only sixty-two. She had been married to Pablo for thirty-five years and always looked so unhappy, even when she smiled. Bonita's words were painful to receive, but even more painful were Hector's words and punches. I hated him, but I didn't know what to do. I was so afraid of him.

The Saturday he let me go with Anita was my reward for keeping my mouth shut about how he really was. Oh, how I wished my life was different.

When I got home, Hector came to the car to help me into the house. He was always about appearances. He always gave people the impression that he was so attentive. Bonita followed. Once inside, the boys were so happy to see me. "Mommy, Mommy, don't leave us again," they said.

When Hector left the room, his sister told me to think about what she had said. "I don't want the next time to be your funeral, Carmen. Your sons need you."

Once Bonita left, Hector told me that there was nothing wrong with me and that he was expecting his meals as usual. "No one's going to baby you, Carmen," he said. I told him what the doctor said, and he said, "I don't care what you do as long as this house is clean, the laundry is done, my food is cooked when I get home, and these boys are taken care of."

A few weeks went by, and everything was pretty much back to normal. After church one Sunday, the boys and I were in the car waiting for Hector. He came over to me and gave me the car keys and said, "You and the boys go home. I'm going over to Caesar's house to hang out with the guys. I'll be home soon." I knew once again he wouldn't be home soon.

The boys and I went home and had a great time. They helped me bake brownies, and then we snuggled on the couch as we watched Bible cartoons. After the boys got their baths, I read a bedtime story to them, kissed them, and said good night. Juan called out to me as I was leaving his and Julio's room. "Mommy, come here." He gave me a hug and squeezed me real tight. "I love you, Mommy. You are better than Papi."

"Why do you say that?" I asked.

"Because you don't hit or yell at Papi. He hits and yells at you." That was a reality check for me. I didn't think the twins realized what was happening. I went in to kiss Hector Jr. and tell him good night. He surprised me too. "Mommy, is it okay to hit girls when they make me mad at school?" he asked.

"No, son, it's never right to hit anyone when they make you angry," I told him.

"Then why does Papi hit you when he is angry?" I didn't know what to say to him, except that we would pray for Papi not to be that way. "Okay," he said.

At ten, I decided to go to bed. I couldn't sleep because I was thinking about what the boys said. I wondered if what Pam Brooks said about some of the men she was trying to help was true of my boys. Were they being affected by Hector's abuse and my letting it continue? I decided to read a bit and then dozed off. When I woke up, it was four thirty in the morning. I looked over to the other side of the bed, and there was no Hector. I knew for sure he was drunk then. My thoughts started again, so I decided to read the scriptures Pastor gave me a while back. While I was reading, my phone rang. There was a frantic man on the other line speaking in Spanish very fast. "Slow down," I told him.

"Your husband has been beaten up real bad and left on your front porch for dead." Then he hung up the phone.

At that point, I wasn't sure if I were dreaming or not. I lay there in bed, deciding whether or not to go see if Hector was on the front porch. A part of me wanted to go look, and another part of me could care less and hoped it was true. Finally, I decided to go check.

As I looked out the window next to the door, I didn't see anyone. I opened the door a bit and still saw no one. As I began to close the door, I heard moaning. I stepped out on the porch, and I saw Hector in the bushes next to the stairs. I turned on the porch light and saw he was bloody and drunk. He smelled of alcohol and cigarettes. He looked to be beaten pretty bad. His eyes were swollen and turning purple. His nose was twisted out of shape, with a cut on the bridge. His face was all scratched up, and there looked to be a long gash on the side of his face and neck. I stood there in shock, wondering what to do. I decided to go back to bed and let Hector figure out his dilemma. As I was walking back up the stairs to my bedroom, I thought about the boys. I didn't want them to see their father like that when the bus and preschool van came to pick them up. They would have to walk right by their father; therefore, I went back and helped him inside. He was in a worse condition than I thought. He cried out in pain every time I tried to move him. I got my neighbor to come stay with the boys while I took Hector to the hospital.

At the hospital, I learned that Hector had three broken ribs as well as a broken nose. He had been cut with something sharp like a knife that left him needing several stitches along the side of his face down to his neck. He had several cuts and bruises. He had to be hospitalized because he was having trouble breathing. They wanted to watch him to prevent the lungs from being punctured by his broken ribs. He was clearly in a great deal of pain. I had never seen Hector like this before. I left him there and went home to pack a bag for him and took it back to the hospital. Hector wanted me to stay, but I told him I had to pick up the boys. Actually, I was glad he had been beaten up. Now he knew what it felt like. I was tired of being the one beaten up. Now it was Hector. I wanted to throw a party every time I heard him moan in pain. I knew this was wrong, but it sure felt good.

A few days later, I decided to call Pamela Brooks. She was so happy to hear from me, and we decided to have lunch. I told her I wanted to talk to her as a woman, not a client. I explained to her what happened to Hector and how happy I was about it. She looked understanding yet saddened by what I had said. I asked her if I was wrong to feel this way. She said it was a natural reaction considering what I had been through.

"Some women would really take advantage of the situation and beat their husbands again and make them suffer more. Others would still be in fear thinking of what he would do when he gets better."

I asked Pam what I should do. She asked me if I had spoken to my pastor about what was going on. I told her no. She suggested that I do that and be honest about everything. I asked her if there was something in her Bible that would help me. She smiled and thought for a moment, reached in her bag, and got her Bible out. To my surprise, she told me about the same scriptures Pastor told me to read: Romans 3:23, John 3:16, and John 10:10. Then she told me I needed to surrender my life to God. I told her that I wanted to, but I didn't know how to do that. Pam told me how she gave her heart to Jesus and thus began her journey of salvation. She explained to me how God loves me so much that he gave his best for me to live and have everlasting life with him.

After she finished explaining that to me, I began to cry. The thought of someone loving me that much was overwhelming. I felt so unworthy of such love. She assured me that I was worthy. For the first time since my teen years, I truly felt special. I told Pam

I wanted to give my life to God and surrender all to him. I asked God to forgive me for being a sinner and to please come live in my heart every day of my life.

When we finished praying, I felt a sense of peace all around me. I no longer hated Hector. I felt pity for him. I wished he could experience what I was at that moment. In my heart, I felt as if someone had opened the door to the cage I had been dwelling in and told me to come out and fly. Now the tears I cried were tears of joy and relief. No one was hugging me, but I felt that same safe and secure feeling I felt when Sister Hernandez embraced me at church. In spite of my life, I felt like I would never have to worry about Hector hitting me again.

I asked Pam, "Is this God making me feel like this?"

She smiled and said, "Yes!"

"Thank you, Pam, for being a friend to me and sharing God's love with me. I understand things a lot more now. I don't think I'm afraid of Hector anymore. I *know* that is God and not me."

We both looked at each other and laughed.

The next morning, I called Pastor Hernandez and told him all about my life with Hector, the abuse and fear, and finally what God did for me when I asked him to live in my heart. He was thrilled about my salvation. He asked if I would mind if he went to the hospital to see Hector, so I told him that was fine.

Later that day, I went to the hospital to see Hector. He seemed to be feeling a bit better, and the swelling in his face was all gone. I told him he was looking better and asked him how he felt. He replied, "I would feel a lot better if you brought my boys to see me. Who is at home with them while you are here?"

"Bonita," I answered. "I hope she hasn't been filling your head with a bunch of crap, Carmen," Hector said. "You will never find anyone who will take care of you like I do. While I was lying here in bed today, I was thinking. This whole thing is your fault, Carmen. Why didn't you call me earlier that evening and tell me to come home? All this would have been avoided if only you would have called me like a good wife. You are so ungrateful after all I've given you." I just stood there in disbelief. "Don't look at me like that, Carmen. You're glad this happened to me. Admit it. I've given you an allowance ever since we were married, bought you a beautiful Chrysler 300, we have a five-bedroom house with a pond in the back, and you and the boys have nice clothes. I lay here in this hospital because of you."

At that point, I could no longer hold back. "You're in this bed because of your self-centered ways. What happened to you is all your fault, not mine, and my sons love me unconditionally. You're the one who doesn't love me, but I found someone who does, and he loves me more than you ever could. He loves me even though you say I'm built like a man. He loves me fat or skinny. He loves me completely for me."

I saw Hector turning red in the face as he asked, "Who are you talking about? When I get out of here, I'll kill him."

"You can't kill him, Hector. You won't want to because he loves you just as much as he loves me," I told him.

"Carmen, who are you talking about? What's his name?"

"His name is Jesus, Hector."

Just then, he tried to laugh but cried out in pain because of his healing ribs against his lungs. "I told you, Carmen, nobody wants you. You have to go and make up an imaginary boyfriend, Jesus. That is funny, but it hurts to laugh, so I won't." Just then, Pastor and Sister Hernandez came into the room. Hector looked amazed.

"Hello, Pastor and Sister Hernandez," Hector said, looking a bit embarrassed. "How long have you been at the door?" he asked cautiously.

Sister Hernandez looked at Hector and then looked at me with sadness in her eyes as she shook her head. Pastor Hernandez said, "Long enough to hear what you said to your wife."

The room was silent for a few seconds, which seemed more

like hours. Hector then said, "I was just kidding with my wife. We always play like that, right, Carmen?"

They all looked at me, waiting for a response. At that moment, so much went through my mind as my leg began to throb a bit from the burn. Whenever I was on my feet awhile, it throbs until I rest awhile. Feeling the pain in my leg and feeling the boldness to stand up to Hector gave me even more courage. So I said, "No, that's not true. He meant every word of what he said. He always puts me down even in front of the boys. He tells me that they don't love me and that I am ugly."

Hector's mouth dropped open as he glared at me. I walked over to him and put my hand on his chin and told him to close his mouth before something flies into it. He looked at Pastor and smiled and said, "That's not true, Pastor. You know how women can be sometimes. I just try to help her. You see all the things God has blessed us with. I don't take any of it for granted."

Pastor asked Hector if he had ever hit me. Once again, the room was silent. He wouldn't answer at first; he just turned his head to look out of the window. Then he asked Pastor if he could speak to him alone. Sister Hernandez and I went to the lounge area.

"Carmen," Sister Hernandez said, "has your husband ever beaten you?"

"Yes," I said, feeling so ashamed. "He told me that I was his property, and he burned me with the iron and said he branded me like I was cattle or something." I showed her the burn on my leg, and she gasped for air.

"He did that to you?"

"Yes, he did, and I hate him. Every time I look at it, I hate him even more. That morning I found him by the porch beaten up, I was going to leave him there. I didn't even care if it would have started to rain on him. To be honest, I was glad he had gotten beaten up. He still doesn't talk about it, so I don't even know what happened or why it happened. Since he has been here in the hospital, the boys and I have had a wonderful time without him. They even said how much fun we have without Papi there."

Sister Hernandez looked at me and said that she understood how I felt. "Now that you have Jesus in your heart, can you forgive Hector for what he has done to you and the boys?"

"Are you kidding? No, no, no! I cannot forgive him. Why should I? Every time I shower or take a bath, I see this scar on my leg. You've seen it. It's ugly."

Sister Hernandez went on to explain. "Carmen, Jesus was beaten too."

"Yeah, I know, he was beaten before he died on the cross."

"Yes, Carmen, but did you know he was branded too?"

"No way!" I said.

"Yes, he was. When the soldiers were beating and making fun of Jesus, they took branches from a thorn bush and made it into a crown. The thorns were at least one inch long. Then they smashed it onto our Savior's head. The thorns penetrated his head and brow. Blood began to run down his head and face. They also drove nails into his wrists and feet. The nails they used were not like our nails today. The nails used were rough, long, thick, and jagged. As if that was not enough, to make sure he was dead, they thrust into his side with a spear.

"All these things left marks on our Savior. The men who did this to our Savior were ordered to do it, but they also took pleasure in doing it. They thought of Jesus as their enemy. They belittled and degraded him. They also stripped him of his clothes and displayed him on the cross for all to see. Now that is total humiliation."

"I didn't know that," I said with tears streaming down my face. "Jesus went through so much more than what I've been through. I guess I really do understand that scripture John 3:16. God *gave* his only *begotten* son to us. Does *begotten* mean that he came from God?"

"Yes, Carmen, you're right," Sister Hernandez continued. "After all that was done to him, he asked our Heavenly Father to forgive them for what they did to him. Remember he was beaten and then whipped with forty lashes as people looked on and cheered. Carmen, do you think that was easy for Jesus to do?"

I held my head down and softly said, "I . . . I don't know."

Sister Hernandez continued, "When we give our hearts to God, he wants them completely so he can give us a new heart in its place. The new heart has the ability to forgive because it is full of God's love. God loves us no matter what we've done. Even if we hate God, he still loves us. His love will clean us inside and help us to forgive. Carmen, do you want to forgive Hector?"

I felt so overwhelmed. I knew it was the right thing to do according to God, but according to me, I just wanted him to hurt more. I told Sister Hernandez, "I want to do the right thing and forgive, but it is hard. Let me think about it. Please pray for me."

"Okay, Carmen, I will pray that God will guide your heart."

We returned to Pastor and Hector, and then I said goodbye and went home. On my way home, I couldn't help but to think about the look Hector gave me before I left. If looks could kill, I would have been dead. He had such hatred in his eyes.

The next day, I spent time with Pam. She took me to a women's shelter, and I talked to some of the women there. Those women took one look at me and knew I had been abused. One woman said to me, "I want what you got, lady! You got the look of a woman who has been beaten down but decided to get back up and live." Another asked me, "How do I get out of this and save myself and my children?" I didn't know what to tell her because I was still in it myself.

Suddenly, Hector called me on my cell phone. I went outside to talk to him. "&*%$!*, why aren't you here? Here I am in the hospital, and you're out somewhere with who knows who and doing who knows what. You need to be at home with those boys. You're a bad mother, Carmen. You don't deserve to have my sons. I want you to come see me. Your place is here with me. I mean it &*%*!"

At that moment, I knew I had to decide. Stay and my life would be the same or worse. If I leave, at least I would have a chance to make a better life for the boys and myself. Now that I asked God to come into my life, I felt so strong and confident. I told Hector, "I'm not coming to see you as long as you talk to me like that. I'm not taking it anymore, Hector. You act like you hate me. I deserve to be treated like a woman, a mother, and a human being. Until you can talk to me and not cuss me, I don't want to talk to you. Goodbye."

When I hung up the phone, I felt like a different woman. My eyes widened, and my mouth dropped open. For a few seconds, I was in shock. Most of all, I was shocked that I didn't feel any fear. Suddenly, I realized Hector was only a man who needed to *know* God, not just *know about* him.

When I went back inside, Pam looked at me and asked, "What happened? You look different, vibrant."

I said, "I guess I just realized I've been born again."

As I lay in bed that night, I began thinking over the recent events of my life. I realized Hector was not going to change anytime soon, and when he came home, he would try to do the same things he did before. Even in the state he was in, he showed no signs of remorse over the way he treated me. He had given me an allowance for several years, and I had always saved it for the day when I would get the courage to leave. I now had almost $55,000 in the savings account I had had since I was fifteen years old. Hector knew nothing about this account. I decided to take the boys and leave Hector. I was not going to go through another beating or allow my sons to see or hear their father beating their mother ever again. This was my chance. Just then, Hector Jr. came and got in bed with me because he said he couldn't sleep. He asked me to read to him from that big black book I always read from. I kissed him on the forehead as he snuggled up to me. I pulled the covers up over us and began to read until he was fast asleep.

The next day, I went to see Pastor and Sister Hernandez and told them I was going to leave Hector. Pastor told me that for the moment, he thought that would be a good idea because Hector has so much hatred inside of him. Pastor said he was concerned for my safety. He also said they were praying for Hector and me and wanted me to be led by God in whatever I do. Sister Hernandez added, "You have our blessing, child."

So I called my sister and her husband in San Diego, California, and they were glad that I was finally leaving him. My brother-in-law told me they were praying for God's will to be done in this whole thing. They said they would help me find an apartment and I could work in my sister's flower shop, keeping her books. She was always bad with numbers. I always got As in math and loved working with numbers. I even took a course in bookkeeping and got a certificate. Pam even connected me with one of the shelters there in San Diego so I could go and volunteer my services to help the women and children there.

I went to the hospital to see Hector, and he told me he would be getting out the next day. I told him I was leaving him and hopefully he would see the need to live his life for God and become a changed man.

He laughed and said, "Stop kidding, Carmen. Where will you go? Nobody wants you." When he saw that I was serious, he said, "You're not taking my boys anywhere. You can go, but they stay. You'll never make it anyway. You'll be back. You have no money and no car 'cause I bought that car. You can't take it. Now how will you make it without me?"

I told him I would make it with the help of God.

He laughed again and said, "Okay, take the boys. Now how

will you make it? You'll have to work and pay bills. With three children, you'll never make it. You'll be back, watch and see. My life will be better with you gone anyway. You are so weak, Carmen."

I looked at Hector, and suddenly, I felt pity for him. I wanted him to get help and become a good man. I wanted him to be a good example for the boys. I asked God to help him.

"Hector, can I pray for you?"

"Yeah, sure, this should be good," he said.

"Father, please help Hector to know who you are for real. God, take care of him and love him. Please forgive him for all the pain he has caused me and the boys. Father, help him to realize that he needs you. I forgive him, God, for yelling, hitting, and kicking me. And for . . . [sobbing] . . . burning my leg."

Hector was quiet. He finally looked at me and said, "You forgive me? What do you mean you forgive me? Carmen, just go wherever it is that you are going and leave me the ^%$# alone."

That was four years ago. Hector Jr. is now nine, and the twins are seven. We are all doing great! I don't regret the decision to get out of that lifestyle. Jesus died for us to have an abundant life through him, not a life of bondage. I still visit that women's shelter in San Diego. In fact, I now own my own shelter for women and children of domestic violence. The boys help out too by playing with the other children who come in. It helps them to feel like kids and keeps their minds off what is going on in the world of their parents. Pam has been a big help as well. She comes to visit from time to time and speaks to the women to encourage them. My sister and brother-in-law volunteer as well as members from our church.

I am also happy to say that Hector, after two years of thinking I was coming back, finally realized that I wasn't. He went through counseling with Pastor Hernandez and, after a year, gave his heart to God. He is doing so much better now, and the boys do spend time with him. The first time I saw him, I noticed he looked so good and happy. However, he has a long scar on the side of his face and neck from the incident that took place years ago that left him on our front porch drunk and bleeding. When I saw it, I thought about the brand he put on me. You could barely see it now. I know God did that because the doctor said I would have an ugly scar for life. When Hector saw me for the first time since I left him, he said, "It looks like I'm the one who got branded for life. This scar reminds me of what I had and how I lost it. It also reminds me of the life I don't want to go back to." He has apologized so many times for all he did to me and the boys. I thank God that he gives us many chances to get it right. Hector said he is in the choir at church and loves to sing for the Lord. Talking to Hector is great now because we actually talk. I am going forward with my life with no promises to Hector. I just want to help as many families as I can. A few of the women and their husbands have gotten back together, and it is working. Most didn't want anything to do with anything that reminded them of that lifestyle.

So I guess all things really do work together for good to those who love God and are called according to his purpose. One of the things I teach the women at the shelter is that there is life after abuse. I tell them that if you are in an abusive relationship, please find someone you can talk to. It can be your pastor, teacher, friend, parent, or anyone who can help you through the word of God. You don't deserve to be physically, verbally, or emotionally abused. God made you to be the head, not the tail, above and not beneath. God loves all of us and doesn't want us to live in abuse.

It's Not Always as it Seems

*For they speak not peace: but they devise deceitful
matters against them that are quiet in the land.*
Psalm 35:20

    I didn't understand why my niece was acting so distant toward me. We had always been so close, closer than sisters. We did everything together: shopping, vacations, dinners, lunches; we even went to the same church. No other aunt and niece could be closer, so why the distance now? When I called her, she was brief and a bit cold. We knew each other so well. I knew something was wrong, but when I asked her about it, she assured me that everything was all right. As time went by, I decided to give our relationship a break. I felt like I was the only one trying anyway to keep the friendship going. *Everyone needs some space*, I thought. So we did our own thing and went our own way. However, I really missed the fun times with Jo (short for Josetta). Our family had a saying about us: "Flo and Jo are always on the go." My name is Florine, but I've been called Flo since I was a child.

    My fiancé, Morey, is a successful executive of a very prominent law firm. He has obtained various awards and degrees that are proudly displayed on his office wall. He is a kind man with a very caring nature. I call him my gentle giant because he is six foot seven, and I am five foot six. Most of all, he loves the Lord and goes with me to church.

One night, Morey and I were having dinner when he asked me how long Jo and I were going to be miserable by not spending time with each other. I asked him why he said that, and he responded, "You two were always doing things together. Now that you aren't, both of you seem so sad." Wow! I didn't know how Jo was doing because I resisted the urge to call her or drop by her condo. Morey told me that I had to deal with this issue even though I didn't know why Jo and I were distant. He said I should do the right thing and confront Jo face-to-face. I was impressed that Morey cared so much and wanted me to be happy, but that was just his way.

The next day, I decided to call Jo, but I didn't know how to start the conversation. To have been close for so long, now it seemed like I was confronting a stranger. I decided to put this whole thing in God's hands and trust him. I wanted my niece back, but most of all, I wanted my best friend back. I asked God to set it all up and work on Jo's heart in the meantime.

One Saturday afternoon, while at home relaxing, someone knocked at my door. To my amazement, it was one of my other nieces, Miranda. I hadn't seen her in about six months. I invited her in and told her how happy I was to see her. After some chitchat, she asked me how Jo was doing. I told her I hadn't spoken to Jo lately.

Miranda told me that she had heard about Jo and I not being close anymore and that I should be glad about it. I was shocked at her statement and asked why I should be happy about it. What came next had to be a lie. She told me that Jo had a one-time fling with my fiancé, Morey, and couldn't face me as a result. Miranda said that Jo felt so bad about it that she just wanted to cut all ties with me. Now she was thinking about going after Morey for herself. She told me that I didn't need Jo in my life because she wasn't a true friend and that family shouldn't do one another that way.

I couldn't hold back the tears, but deep down, I knew this couldn't be true, could it? Morey never gave any indication or signals that anything was wrong. Surely, I would have known if something was wrong.

Then Miranda said, "Morey told Jo to cool the relationship with you because it was awkward and uncomfortable for him."

As she was talking, I interrupted her and told her to stop. I couldn't take any more of what she was saying. She embraced me and said that I didn't need either of them and that she would be there for me now. I felt like a ton of bricks had just fallen on me. Miranda left, but before she did, she told me that she was sworn to secrecy and that I shouldn't tell anyone what she had told me. I was numb and really wasn't paying attention to what she was saying at this point. It was as if I was frozen in the thoughts of my mind.

I sat there for hours, going over what Miranda had just told to me. The more I went over it, the worse it seemed to get. My mind was reeling. When did this happen? Now I knew why Jo couldn't face me. I couldn't believe Morey would do such a thing. We were so in love with each other. I know things happen to people, but not to us, not this. Why, why, why? How could they? After pondering, crying, and reflecting, I decided to call Morey and get to the bottom of this.

As I reached for the phone, I saw a magazine on the table with my mail entitled *In the Potter's Hand*. On the cover, one word seemed to jump out at me—*forgiveness*. I picked up the magazine and paged through it. One article spoke about the number of times we are to forgive someone according to the Bible. As I read, my vision got blurred because of the tears. How could I forgive Jo and Morey for what they did? In fact, how could I even forgive Miranda for telling me about it? It was so much easier to hate them all, but what would that do to me?

All of a sudden, I thought, *How do I know she told me the truth? Miranda could have made the whole thing up.* But that didn't make any sense; she had nothing to gain or lose as a result. The hurt I felt was deeper than anything I had ever experienced before, but I decided at that moment to forgive like it said in the magazine. I told God I wanted to forgive, but it was hard for me, so I asked him to help me. If it were not true, I still needed to forgive Miranda for causing such pain. While kneeling down at my couch, talking to God and giving it over to him, I heard Jo's voice outside. I got up to look out of my window, and I saw Jo and Morey outside my house talking to each other. Apparently, they pulled up at the same time. *How convenient*, I thought. As I opened my door, I asked God to help me to do and say the right things.

When I stepped out on my porch, I saw Morey holding Jo in an embrace. I began to fume. As I made my way to where they were, Jo saw me coming. She must have told Morey because he quickly turned around in my direction and stepped away from her. At that moment, I wanted to tell God to close his eyes and shut his ears for about ten minutes so I could deal with them. I could feel my old ways coming back. In the old days, I would have jumped on Morey and slapped, kicked, and punched Jo. Then I would have thought of a way to get even and cause them the same pain they caused me. Jo began to back away from Morey as I stepped up to them. She saw the rage in my face. I looked at them both and asked, "What's going on here?"

Morey said, "Sweetie, Jo came over to try to get things straight with you and asked me to come for moral support."

"Is that what they're calling it these days, 'moral support'?"

Morey looked bewildered. "What?" he said. I wanted to open my mouth and let go some words that God surely wouldn't have been pleased with. All of a sudden, Jo interrupted.

"Flo, please listen to what I have to say. I'm sorry I've been so distant with you, but hear me out, please!" I could feel my ears getting hot from anger.

Morey took my hand and said, "Baby, what's wrong? I've never seen you like this before."

I said, "I've never felt this way before, and I never knew I could feel such pain and anger."

He replied, "Can we all go inside and talk?" I consented, and we all went inside my house to the den, where the atmosphere was more relaxed.

I sat in my recliner, and they sat on the couch. This way I could see them and their reactions to what was about to be said. I had an earful for them.

Morey said, "Let's pray before we start this conversation."

I looked up at him in shock and said, "Pray? Don't be getting all holy on me now, what's up with that?"

Morey looked at me and said, "Flo, you don't think I've been going to church with you all this time just to be close to you, do you?" He laughed and continued, "I must admit at first I did. I am a man of goals, and one of them was to get you into bed, but as I listened to the messages, I began to realize that all my awards and recognitions were nothing without God. I've learned a lot and made some changes in my life as a result."

Man, why did he have to go and say all that? Now I was feeling kind of bad, but at the same time, I was seeing a new man in Morey. One I liked even more. Wow, this was nice, but that did not make me forget the issue at hand.

I said, "What's going on between you two?"

Jo spoke first. "Flo, did Miranda come by to see you?"

I looked at her with the look of "you got some nerve" and replied, "No, Jo, you aren't asking the questions here. Just answer them. You owe me an explanation. In fact, you both do, and I want it now!"

Jo dropped her head and said, "You're right, I do. I have been so ashamed of myself for shutting you out of my life, Flo."

I glared at Jo and said coldly, "And what have you done to be ashamed of, Jo?" I carefully watched Jo as she began.

"Remember that promotion I was up for on my job, which would have made me assistant to the president of the company? Well, as you know, I got it and all the perks that comes with it. My bank account has never been so fat, my condo looks fabulous, my ride is smooth, and I wear the best and eat at the best places. My life had never been so great. One day, I stayed at work late to get a head start on some new accounts I was introducing to the company the next day. Walter Briggs, my boss and the president of the company, came into my office. He told me how happy he was that I had gotten the promotion and what an asset I was being to the company. He told me I was his right hand. He wanted to hear my presentation, so I shared it with him. He critiqued it, and it was all good."

I interrupted, "Jo, this is all good, but what does this have to do with you and Morey?"

"What? What are you saying, Flo?" Morey said as he looked at me in amazement.

Jo interrupted, "Wait, Flo, hear me out! Please listen to everything before you say anything! My boss threatened my job if I didn't have sex with him."

I was horrified by what Jo said. At that moment, I became the aunt, not the friend, and wanted to go deal with Mr. Walter Briggs myself.

Then Jo continued, "When I refused, he made my job miserable. He told me he was the president and he had the last say overall and no one could override his word. I panicked, Flo. I was still paying for my new lifestyle and couldn't afford to lose my job. I felt trapped, so I did what he wanted me to do." Jo hung her head down and began to cry so hard, her body began to shake. "I was so ashamed I couldn't face anyone, not even you, Flo. I loved my job, but now I hate it because of Walter. I'm good at my job, and I've put everything into it. I've worked hard to get this far, and the price for it is my body. It's not fair," Jo said.

I went over to hug her and held her as if she were a baby, my baby. "I'm so sorry, Jo. I had no idea," I replied.

Just then, Morey said, "Honey, it tore me up to see you and Jo so sad and not speaking, so I tried to get you two to talk to each other. I called Jo one afternoon and asked her if I could come by after I got off from work that evening. She hesitated until I told her I needed to talk to her about you. She thought something had happened to you, Flo, and told me I could come by. Once I arrived at Jo's condo, I saw she was a very fragile woman. I'd never seen her that way before. She was always so strong, so confident. The woman I was looking at was beaten down and worn with worry. Before I could say anything, she wanted to know what was going on with you, Flo. She said she was worrying about you ever since I called her to see if I could come by. I asked why she didn't call you anymore or go by your house. Getting her to answer my questions was like pulling teeth that weren't loose. Finally, she told me the story she just told you, and she began to weep. I spoke to her about pressing charges and referred her to one of my colleagues who is familiar with these types of cases."

Jo began to speak. "I was afraid to take Morey's advice. After all, we weren't just talking about sexual harassment, but we were talking about my career as well. I told him to let me take some time to think about things.

"As I walked him out to his car, he was saying some really encouraging things to me. It made me think of how you used to encourage me about my life and letting God into it. I told him thank you, and he hugged me. At that moment, I broke down and cried for two reasons. One, I knew he was genuinely concerned about me. Two, this was one good man, and I was so happy you two were getting married. I felt you two deserve each other.

"So I avoid Walter at work as much as possible and never stay longer than I have to. Today, I went to my gynecologist for my annual exam. While there, I found out I have gonorrhea and syphilis. Now I have to have treatments to be cured. Do you know how embarrassing that is? If that wasn't bad enough, when I came out of the doctor's office, Miranda was walking in. She asked me what I was doing there. I was still in shock by what the doctor told me about my condition that I didn't know what to say to her. Suddenly, she asked if it had anything to do with Morey. I was surprised by that question and asked why she would ask such a thing. She told me she saw Morey and me outside my condo hugging and kissing. I told her he was not kissing me; he was just being a friend consoling me. She told me I was lying and asked me what I thought you would think about it. She called me a backstabbing, two-faced tramp. She also told me she never liked how close I was to you and this was her opportunity to break up our relationship. She said she would become your best friend now. When I got to my car, I thought I was going to have a nervous breakdown. I didn't understand why all this was happening to me. I never did anything to Miranda except love her. When we were little girls, we used to spend the night over each other's houses all the time. We grew up close and then went our separate ways when we went to different high schools. She had her friends, and I had mine, but the love was still there. When I got home from the doctor, I called Morey and told him what Miranda said. He told me that now was the time to tell you before you heard the wrong thing from Miranda."

Then I said, "Well, it's too late for that. She already came by and told me that you two had an affair with each other and that you, Jo, now wanted Morey for yourself. Jo, why didn't you tell me this before? I thought we could tell each other anything."

Jo responded, "I really admire you and your life and wanted to be like you. You seem to have it all together. You were always telling me how Jesus loves me and died for me and wants me in his family. Well, when all that happened, I felt like no one wanted me, not even Jesus. I felt so dirty, and I wanted to die. Last night, I was going to kill myself. I knew I needed to pay my bills, and if I quit, I'd have no money to take care of things. Each time I thought of Walter putting his hands on me, I felt so filthy. I found myself taking two or more showers a day. Then I realized that I couldn't wash away the filth I was feeling because it was coming from inside. I knew if I reported Walter and brought him up on sexual harassment charges, I'd be out of a job anyway because it would be so uncomfortable there with all the whispers. I felt like I couldn't take it anymore. I dialed your number, but when I got to the last digit, I hung up. I was so ashamed, Flo. I didn't want you to see me as a failure. You and Morey were always so happy and living a good Christian life. I wanted that too. I just didn't want to give up the pleasures of . . . well, my sinful life." Jo smiled softly and continued, "I felt that if I were close to you, somehow I would get into heaven when I die. When all this happened, I felt so alone. You know that peace you're always talking about? I couldn't feel it. I needed it so bad, but it wasn't there. You and Morey always speak of peace that passes all understanding. I wish I knew that. My life is in such chaos." Jo hung her head down and said, "Maybe I am a tramp like Miranda said."

As I listened to Jo, I began to feel bad for the way I had been thinking and feeling. I grabbed her shoulders and said to her, "Jo, you're not a tramp. Don't ever think that about yourself. Miranda doesn't know what you've been through. If she did, she never would have said that." I told them about my visit with Miranda and asked them to forgive me. I also told them I forgive Miranda too. Jo looked at me and asked how I could forgive her after what she had done. I told her I was reminded of the goodness of the

Lord and how important he is and has been in my life. He has brought me far from my old ways. I was reacquainted with some of them tonight and realized I still have stuff to get out of me. The only way I can do that is to repent of those old thoughts and submit them to God. I told Jo, "No one is perfect, and no matter how good it seems, there is always better in God. Baby, give your heart to him and let him handle your situation. God knows how to handle this. Put Walter Briggs in his very capable hands and let him work it out for you. Only he knows the way because he is the way."

Jo began to cry again and said she was so glad she listened to Morey. We all held hands, and I led Jo to her new life in Christ. Afterward, I called Miranda and asked her to come by again.

When she arrived, she was shocked to see Morey and Jo there. Immediately, she went into a rage and said, "I told you not to tell them. I can't trust you."

We explained to her that what she thought she saw was not the truth and told her how damaging and destructive the lie she told could have been. She was not happy and started yelling, "How can you believe them over me? They betrayed you, Flo. I'm the only one you can trust." I told her she didn't know all the details. With a smirk on her face, Miranda said, "I know what I need to know, and that is that you all deserve each other. I'm sure Morey will like that."

Before I knew it, Jo slapped her. Miranda went to hit her back, and I caught her hand. I said to her, "Miranda, I know you're not implying anything vulgar. What have I done to you that would make you want to hurt me like this?"

As Miranda snatched her hand from me, she said, "I just wanted to be cool with you too. Sometimes you need a third party to open your eyes to what is real."

All I could do was look at her for a moment and shake my head. Finally, I said, "Miranda, you need help. What you told me was not real, can't you see that? You caused so much pain, and someone could have gotten hurt."

Jo said, "Yeah, like I feel like hurting you right now, but I won't because I have a new life. But make no mistake, Miranda, cousin or no cousin, I've just started this new life, and the old me is still pretty fresh."

Miranda turned to walk out, but Morey stopped her.

"Miranda," Morey said, "what's really wrong? You said you wanted to be close to Flo. You can be. Jo is your cousin. You're all family, and this is crazy. You shouldn't be fighting like this. Don't leave upset. Let's try to work it out."

Miranda glared at Morey. "Why should I?"

Morey said, "Because you love your aunt and she loves you. You will regret it if you leave without working this out. Make peace, Miranda."

I walked over to her and hugged her and told her I loved her and nothing could stop that. She looked at me in shock.

Miranda asked, "Why?"

I said, "Because you are my niece, girl!"

Jo took my cue and said, "I'm sorry I slapped you, Miranda. That was not the right way to handle this. I haven't had an affair with anyone." Jo explained to Miranda a bit of what happened to her. Miranda felt so bad for misjudging her and for taking advantage of the situation.

"Okay, Jo, now that I have a better understanding of what I saw, it makes sense. I'm sorry for causing you all so much pain. I didn't think it would turn out like this. I was being selfish and wanted to have a relationship like Aunt Flo and Jo. I feel really bad now, Jo. I'm sorry about what has happened to you, girl. I didn't mean to add to your pain." Miranda hugged Jo and said, "You are different! Maybe I can go to church with you sometime."

"That would be great, Miranda. Just let me know whenever

you want to come. You're welcome to come with me anytime," Jo said. Then I hugged them both, and my Morey stood back, watching with the biggest smile on his face.

Two weeks later, Jo called me and said, "Flo, you'll never guess what happened. The police came to the office and arrested Walter today. Apparently, there have been several complaints against him, mine included. So they began to investigate and watch him. He was caught with his pants down, literally! He was trying to make my assistant, Shelly, do something, and he forgot to lock the door. In walked the nighttime security officer. *Bam.* He was caught with his pants around his ankles. She was kneeling down in front of him with tears streaming down her face as he was saying to her, 'Do it now, Shelly, or I'll fire you!' She pressed charges, and then you wouldn't believe what happened next. *Six* other women came forward, all from the office. He must have been doing this for quite some time."

I responded, "Wow, look at how God is working all this out. He's not finished yet, Jo. God never starts something without finishing it. You watch and see, girl."

Three days later, Jo called again. "Walter pled guilty to all charges and has to serve time. Here's the best part, Flo. Guess what, they made me president of the company! The decision was unanimous. I'm so glad I listened to you and Morey and gave my life to God and let him handle this whole thing."

"Congratulations, Jo! I'm so happy for you! That's great news. God sure has turned this whole thing around. We need to celebrate."

"Yeah, I know, Flo. I want to take you, Morey, and Miranda out to dinner on me. I'm so happy."

"That would be great, Jo. Count me in."

"Hey, Flo."

"Yeah, Jo?"

"I love you, girl, and thank God for you."

"I love you too, sweetie! Oh, by the way, Morey and I have set the date to get married. It's September 26. Will you be my maid of honor, Jo?"

"Of course, Flo, I'd be honored to be your maid of honor. I've learned so much from you and Morey. Nothing would give me greater pleasure than to be there for the two of you. Hey, don't forget, we're having lunch and going shopping on Saturday. Flo, you want to invite Miranda to come with us?"

"Yeah, Jo, that sounds like it'll be fun. You know, Jo, sometimes it's really amazing how things work out. Anyway, girl, gotta go, Jo. Someone is at my door. Love ya, girl!"

"Love you too, Flo. Bye."

At my door stood the most handsome man in the whole world—Morey. "Hi, honey, come on in." I had prepared dinner for us, so we went into the dining room where the table was beautifully set in ivory and gold.

I brought Morey up-to-date on what happened to Jo. He was so happy and said, "The scripture is true, Flo. 'All things work out together for the good of those who love God and to those who are called according to his purpose.' Wow, this is a real lesson in trust. Now no one could ever convince Jo that God is not real. She has her own experience to say otherwise."

"Morey, on Saturday, Jo and I are going to spend the day together, having lunch and then going shopping. We decided to invite Miranda to come with us. I know she will come, and it will be a lot of fun. God is so good, baby."

After dinner, we went into the kitchen to wash dishes. While washing dishes, I said, "Morey?"

He replied, "Yeah, baby?"

"I'm so glad God gave me you. I'm so proud of what I see happening in your life. You were the man who took charge when Jo, Miranda, and I were fussing with one another. I'm so glad you were there, took control, and got Miranda to stay, and as a result, we all worked things out. You've really grown into a strong man of God, my man of God! I love you."

Morey grabbed my soapy hand and kissed the back of it, leaving soap on his face. He smiled and said, "I love you too, Flo."

Jealousy: A Silent Killer

> And Esau hated Jacob because of the blessing
> wherewith his father blessed him: and Esau said in
> his heart, the days of mourning for my father are
> at hand; then will I slay my brother Jacob.
> Genesis 27:41

"Why did she do it?" Hank asked through his tears. "Why? She had everything in front of her. How could my baby do this to herself?"

I reached out to comfort my husband as we sobbed uncontrollably. Our youngest child, Jan, who was only seventeen, killed herself. It made no sense to us. She seemed happy and was her usual humorous self. Wherever Jan was, there was bound to be laughter. When she walked into a room, she brought fun with her. A party was not a party until Jan got there. Our son, Justin, who was twenty, came to our bedroom door and told us everyone was looking for us.

"Hank, honey, we've got to go downstairs to mingle with the people. They came to pay their respect to Jan and to support us. The funeral is over, and all we have to do is get through this. Then we can begin to sort through all this, okay?"

"You go, Martha. I can't be around anyone now. I . . . I just can't handle it." I kissed Hank and hugged him and told him to take his time. I went down to mingle with our family and friends.

As I was walking past Jan's bedroom, I heard voices inside. I pushed the door open to find her best friend, Stacey; boyfriend, Jeff; and classmate Carla in her room.

Stacey was sitting on Jan's bed, holding a picture of her and Jan having fun at the water park. While she was looking at the picture, she mumbled, "She was a real Christian. I want to be more like her."

Jeff was sitting on the floor, hugging the huge stuffed bear he gave Jan on her seventeenth birthday, and Carla was reminiscing about the times they all had together with Jan.

Jeff was crying and said, "It never should have happened like this. Not to Jan." I walked in and startled them.

Stacey said, "We're sorry, Mrs. B [short for Baxter]. I hope you aren't mad at us for being in Jan's room. It's just that whenever we were here, this was where we hung out. It seems strange now being here without Jan saying something funny and making us all laugh." Then she began to cry.

I went over to comfort her and told them all that if Jan were here now, she would find a way to make everyone laugh in the midst of their sorrow. They all smiled and laughed a bit and then agreed.

"Can we hang out here for a while, Mrs. B? We don't really want to be downstairs with everyone else. Being in Jan's room kinda makes us feel like she's here with us."

"Sure, I guess that will be fine, but not for too long. And don't mess up anything. I want it to stay the way she left it for the time being."

"Thank you, Mrs. B," Jeff said as he came over to hug me.

I went downstairs and visited with our guests and expressed an excuse for my husband's absence. Everyone understood and felt I was really being strong. I told them I had to be for everyone else.

I went in the kitchen where my other daughter, Jessica, who was nineteen, was getting more cake to put out on the table.

"Are you all right, honey?" I said as I pushed her hair back from her face.

"No, Mom, I'm not all right! This just doesn't make sense. Jan was happy! Why would she do this? I don't believe she's gone. It has to be a bad joke someone is playing on us! Mom, this just can't be real!"

"Jessica, I know it doesn't seem real, and I don't want it to be real. If only we could go back in time, I would find a way to get her to tell me what was on her mind so she wouldn't feel like ki-ki—I can't even say it." I reached out to hug Jessica, but she resisted.

"I've got to take this cake inside."

I was shocked. No, this wasn't going to destroy my family. I heard that these types of things have torn families apart, but it wasn't going to get my family. No way!

Later, after everyone had left, Hank came down and wanted the whole family to gather in the family room. After we were all settled, it was quiet for a brief moment.

Hank spoke. "I want all of you to know how much I love you. There isn't anything I wouldn't do for my family. I want you to know that."

"We know that, Dad," Justin said. "You have always been there for us even when we didn't know you were there, like at our games, recitals, or plays at school."

Jessica spoke up. "Yeah, Dad, Justin is right. We all know you have always been there for us ever since I can remember. That's why it doesn't make sense to me for Jan to kill herself. You and Mom are always here for us!"

Then Hank said, "I want us to always talk to one another. During times like this, so many families fall apart. I don't want that for my family. We must be strong and hold one another up. Jan would want that for us."

Then I said, "Right about now, she would have chimed in with something funny to break the mood and make us all laugh."

Then Jessica came over and sat by me and said, "I'm sorry, Mom, for getting an attitude with you. I just can't believe you are accepting what they are saying about Jan. I know it seems like she killed herself, but she didn't. She couldn't have. She was too happy and excited about life! We spoke the day it happened, and she was talking about how one day we were going to be moms and have husbands and children. We talked about our children playing together and how we would get you and Dad to babysit while we ditch our husbands and go to Tahiti to lie on the beach and shop. Jan said she hoped we would be great parents like you and Dad. Dad, she also said she wanted to marry someone just like you."

Hank broke into tears again. By now, Jess was crying but managed to say through her tears, "Does that sound like someone who was planning to kill herself just hours later?" I began to cry, and Justin came over and held me. Hank went over to embrace Jess, and we all had that big cry. We did this together as a family, just us.

The next morning, I woke up and found Hank already awake. He was sitting up in bed, thinking. "Good morning, honey," I said.

Hank leaned over to kiss me. "Good morning, baby."

"Whatcha doing? Did you get any sleep last night?" I asked.

"I slept okay. I've been thinking about what Jess said Jan told her the day she died. That doesn't sound like something someone would say if they were planning to commit suicide. I'm starting to feel like Jess now."

"Well, Hank, if it bothers you that much, and I must admit it does make sense, let's pray about it."

Hank responded, "Thanks, honey, for standing with me on this."

Then we prayed, "Lord, thank you for this day and all that you have for us today. We give you this day and ask that your will be done on earth according to your will in heaven. Lord, thank you for taking care of our baby Jan. God, she was so young! We know she is with you now, Father, and ask that you help us to heal. Oh, God, please take away this pain! We miss our baby! It's so hard for all of us to accept because things just don't add up. Father, reveal the truth to us and take care of this whole thing. Thank you for our friends and family who are standing by us. Bless them, Lord. Somehow fill our hearts with your joy again and give us peace. Keep us close and protect us all in Jesus's name, Amen."

Later that day, Jess and I went in Jan's room to just feel her. I opened her closet and touched her clothes. I saw her favorite outfit, closed my eyes, and held it to my face and smelled her fragrance. *Wow*, I thought, *this is like having her here.*

Jess broke the moment by saying, "Mom, look!" She had Jan's journal and showed me that some pages had been torn out.

"What's this?" I said.

"Mom, look, the pages torn out are the last ones she wrote." Jess and I looked at each other, and both said, "Why?" Jess continued. "Mom, I know this has something to do with her death. I just want to know why she tore these pages out and what she did with them."

I thought for a moment and said, "Jess, honey, you know yesterday Stacey, Jeff, and Carla were in here. They said they couldn't take being downstairs with everyone else and wanted to know if they could stay in Jan's room awhile. They said it made them feel as if she were still here. I didn't see anything wrong with it and said yes but told them not to mess with her things. I wonder if they looked at her journal."

At that moment, Justin called for us to come downstairs. When we arrived downstairs, Hank said he had just gotten off the phone with Detective Swift. He and his partner, Detective Sweeney, wanted to know if they could come by, and Hank told them yes. "They should be here in ten minutes. He said he had some news for the family and wanted to talk to all of us," Hank said.

It was silent for a few seconds as we all stared at one another. "How did he sound?" I asked.

Hank replied, "He sounded like he had something on his mind."

Once the detectives arrived, we showed them into the family room. I watched them as their eyes went all around the room examining all the photos, smiling and commenting on them.

Detective Swift said, "You all really seem like a close family."

"We are," Hank replied. "Have a seat, Detectives Sweeney and Swift. This is my wife, Martha; my son, Justin; and my daughter Jessica."

"Hello, we're so sorry for your loss. Let me first express our deepest sympathy," Detective Swift said.

"Thank you," I replied. Detective Swift sat on the couch and took out a small notebook and pencil while Detective Sweeney observed our every movement. "What's this all about?" Hank asked.

"Mr. Baxter, there was something about your daughter's suicide that didn't sit right with me. Everyone else said it was a simple case of suicide. I disagreed and still do. I had no proof, but in my gut, something wasn't right. Now we have proof." I reached out to grab Hank's hand and squeezed it tight and held my breath for a moment. Detective Swift continued, "The bullet that killed your daughter doesn't match the gun used in the suicide. The gun we found at the scene was not the same gun used to kill your daughter. I'm sorry to tell you that this is now a murder investigation." Everyone seemed to be frozen for what seemed like eternity. "Now I need to know anything from you all that might help us in this investigation. The slightest little thing could be a clue."

Jess spoke up. "I never did think Jan did that to herself." She began to relay to the detective the story she told us. He thought that was quite interesting and said that was not characteristic of someone planning to commit suicide. She also told him about the torn pages out of her journal. He asked if he could see the journal and keep it for examination. I asked if we could get it back, and he said we could after the investigation. Detective Swift asked us questions, and we answered them all to the best of our ability. All the while Detective Sweeney was the silent observer.

As they were leaving, I thought about the kids who stayed up in Jan's room the day of the funeral. I said, "I don't think there's anything to this, but after the funeral, everyone came to the house. I was upstairs, and as I passed Jan's room, I heard her friends inside. I went in and was surprised to find them there. They asked me if they could stay there because it made them feel as if Jan was still with them. I didn't see any harm in it, so I told them yes."

"Mrs. Baxter, who were these kids?" I told him who they were, and he wrote their names in his notebook. Then he said, "It probably is nothing, but I must follow up on everything. Thank you, Mr. and Mrs. Baxter, for all your help. As soon as we find out something worth reporting, we'll be in touch to let you know what we've found. In the meantime, here is my card if anything else comes to mind." He gave Jess and Justin a card too.

After they left, we all gathered in the kitchen and just stood around in an ice-cold silence. It was as if time was standing still. Suddenly, Justin punched a hole in the wall with his fist and screamed out, "Why?" I don't think it really hit us until then. Our sorrow quickly turned to anger. Who would want to hurt Jan? Everyone loved her. It just didn't make sense.

Hank hugged Justin and said, "Son, we don't know why this happened, but we will understand it better as time goes by. God will reveal—"

Justin interrupted Hank, "I don't want to hear anything about God. Why did he let it happen in the first place? He is God. He has control, right? Then why didn't he stop this from happening?"

Hank hung his head down and said, "I don't know, son. I just don't know. But we've got to stay together. Okay?" He held Justin tight in his arms as Justin cried again. "I love you, son. I love you more than you'll ever know, and we'll get through this."

As the next few days passed, we were all rather quiet. We weren't really sure what was going on with the investigation, so I decided to call Detective Swift to see if there were any leads. I told him we hadn't heard anything, so I thought I'd call to see how things were going. He told me that they were moving forward in the investigation and that things were coming together. Detective Swift also informed me that as soon as they knew something concrete, he'd call me personally. Then he said, "Mrs. Baxter, off the record, I want you to know that I have a seventeen-year-old daughter too. She is a lot like the way you all described Jan. That's why it just didn't make sense to me why this bright, vibrant girl would kill herself. I just couldn't let it go. I'm glad I didn't. Jan needs someone to fight for her, and I'm doing that."

I happily responded, "God bless you, Detective. You have a seventeen-year-old daughter too? What's her name?" He told me her name was Kira. "Thank you again, Detective, for taking a personal interest in this and for fighting for Jan. God will lead you to the truth. We're praying for you," I told him.

He thanked me and asked if we were a Christian family, and I told him that we were. With excitement in his voice, he said, "Then it is more than an honor to help you and your family. Detective Sweeney and I are Christians too. We need your prayers and appreciate them. We see so much in our line of work. Being homicide detectives is sometimes a very difficult job. We touch so many families."

Then I replied, "I know it must be difficult at times, but just remember God is with you always, even when you are in awkward or difficult situations. Thank you again, Detective."

"No problem, Mrs. Baxter. Goodbye."

"Goodbye, Detective Swift."

I told Hank and the kids that the detectives God put on the

case were Christians, and that seemed to bring a sense of peace to all our hearts except Justin. He was still very angry with God. As time continued to pass, we got stronger. Hank called us all together once a week for a time to read the Bible and be encouraged through God's word. This not only helped us with the healing and anger but also kept us close as a family. It was taking a lot longer for Justin, but he was beginning to come around too. We held one another when we needed it, and slowly, we began to laugh more. Then we noticed it was easier to talk about Jan and laugh at the memories of her sense of humor. Every now and then, Stacey called to see how we all were doing and to let us know how she was doing. We didn't hear much from Jeff. I guess it was too hard for him, and to move on, he had to let go of the past. I never heard from Carla since the day of the funeral. Our family and church family really helped us get through the difficult first stages of Jan's death and kept us encouraged throughout. You never think that when you are a parent, you will have to bury your child; you expect them to bury you.

Ten Months Later

I'll never forget that day, September 23. The phone rang at 4:38 p.m. It was Detective Swift with news about the investigation. He wanted to come by to talk with Hank and me.

When he walked in the door, my heart felt like it sank. I knew this moment would come, but how do you prepare for something like this? Hank and I purposely didn't call Justin and Jessica there because we wanted to be the ones to tell them whatever we were about to be told, and though Justin had come a long way, he still had anger issues. I wasn't sure what he might do if we ever found out who killed Jan. Before the detective arrived, Hank and I prayed for wisdom and asked God to guide our hearts.

"Mr. and Mrs. Baxter, we have information about Jan's death,"

Detective Swift said. "We've been questioning and requestioning various individuals with no leads. Everything seemed so airtight. So we decided to just let things lie for a while, hoping someone would come forward with something. Yesterday, we got a breakthrough. One of the kids at Jan's school began dating a guy who attends Lancaster University. As they got closer in their relationship, the young lady needed someone to confide in. She told this guy that she needed someone to talk to because she was being eaten alive with guilt and felt she would explode if she didn't tell someone. The young man said she tried to convince him to run away with her, but he talked her out of it. She made him swear he'd never tell, but once he heard the story, he felt he had to come forward. He said they just started dating a month and a half ago and were getting pretty serious fast when she decided to tell him. This young lady was apparently very jealous of Jan. He said she secretly desired to be like her. She even began wearing her hair like Jan and tried to act like her. She said that she began flirting with Jan's boyfriend, Jeff, and that she was very careful not to do this in front of Jan but said somehow she always found out. Then Jan and Jeff began to have arguments over this girl. She told the young man that Jan's popular, good girl image was overrated and said she would give Jeff what he deserved. She tried to seduce Jeff on numerous occasions. Jeff and Jan argued a lot but were beginning to work things out. She saw she was losing and wanted Jeff for herself. She tricked Jan by using a mutual friend to lure her to the school's track field."

Then I broke in and said, "Oh yes, I remember Jan calling me and telling me she was going to meet—" Just then, my eyes widened in disbelief. "No . . . no . . . it can't be. Stacey?"

"Yes, Mrs. Baxter. She was used to lure Jan to the track field. I don't know her story yet. Detective Sweeney is at the station now with her and the other kids."

"What other kids?" Hank asked.

"Well, let me finish, Mr. Baxter, and it will all make sense. Stacey got Jan to meet her at the track field while this other young lady was there waiting to confront her. Once Jan got there, she and Stacey started to jog around the track when this other girl came up to them and told Jan she didn't like her. Jan asked her why and what she did to make her dislike her. One thing led to another, and the girl nervously pulled out a gun and told her to go with her out in the wooded area by the track. Jan went, and that was where she was shot, and the girl switched guns. She put another gun in Jan's hand and pulled the trigger so we would find powder burns on Jan's hand. She took the real gun and said she put it back in her father's gun collection. That was not hard to trace because she did not clean the gun. We checked, and the bullet that killed Jan matched that gun in her father's collection. Mr. and Mrs. Baxter, this is the hard part. You know the girl."

"Who is she?" I asked as anger rose in me. This time, Hank took my hand and squeezed it.

"It is Carla Jones."

My knees got weak, and I fell against Hank, who caught me as I began to drop. "Carla? Carla?" I said. As the thoughts were racing through my mind, I said, "She must have taken the pages from Jan's journal."

"Yes, she did," Detective Swift said. "Apparently, Jan wrote about what was happening between them all, and Carla saw it in her journal and tore the pages out so no one would suspect her. I would like for you two to come with me down to the station where the kids are now. Carla has already been taken into custody. She confessed to the whole story. Are you up to this, Mr. and Mrs. Baxter?"

"Yes!" I said without consulting Hank.

"Are you all right, Mrs. Baxter?" Detective Swift said.

"No, Detective, I'm not. I knew this day would come, and I thought I'd be ready when it did. But I don't think you could ever be ready to find out the truth concerning who killed your daughter."

Detective Swift replied, "I think I understand, Mrs. Baxter. I'm so sorry about all this."

Hank said, "It's like starting all over again. Only this time, I feel peace in the midst of it all. Honey, God has brought us this far. He will take us the rest of the way. I love you, Martha." Hank held me tight.

I turned to look at Detective Swift. "Thank you for fighting for Jan, Detective. You said you would, and you did. God bless you and Detective Sweeney as well as everyone else who helped Jan tell us what really happened." I turned back to Hank and rested my head gently on his chest and cried softly.

He rested his head on top of mine and said, "The truth is being revealed, honey. God is answering our prayers."

We left a note for Justin and Jessica and accompanied Detective Swift to the station. There it all unfolded. We saw the gun, met the young man who came forward, and saw Stacey, Carla, and Jeff. I asked Detective Sweeney if Jeff had anything to do with Jan's death. He told us Jeff was innocent and so sorry it all led to Jan's death.

Detective Sweeney said, "He took it very hard, Mrs. Baxter. He felt he should have seen it coming and saved her. He really loved your daughter."

Hank and I were relieved to hear that. Jeff used to come to church with us all the time. When he saw us, he seemed as if he wasn't sure what to do. Hank went over to him and said, "We still love you, Jeff. Thanks for loving our daughter the way you did."

"I still do, Mr. B. It won't go away," Jeff said.

Hank embraced Jeff, who began to cry. I went over and embraced him too. "Jeff, you are always welcome at our house. But if you aren't ready to come by yet, we understand."

Jeff thanked us and said he'd still like to go to church with us because he really missed it. Hank told Jeff to let us know when he was ready and we'd pick him up.

Next, we saw Stacey. When she saw us, she was so ashamed she couldn't look us in the face. Detective Sweeney told us that although she lured Jan to the track field, she was not aware of what Carla intended to do. Once things began to happen, they got out of control, and Carla told Stacey she was just as guilty as she was. Stacey was scared; she said she wanted to tell but was afraid of what would happen.

Hank asked if we could talk to her. They allowed us to speak to Stacey. "Stacey," I said, "I don't pretend to understand what happened that day because I don't. Jan trusted you. How could you trick her like that?"

Stacey began to cry. "I didn't know what Carla was going to do, Mrs. B. You've got to believe me. I was so scared. I just didn't know what to do. I loved Jan like a sister. I still miss her so much. You don't know how many times I wished I could go back to that day."

Hank interrupted, "Stacey, this is why we need to think before we act. Did you know Carla really didn't like Jan? If you really loved Jan, why would you let Carla talk you into that? You were like a daughter to us, Stacey. You spent half the time at our house, and the other half Jan was at your house. Jan loved you so much."

Stacey began to cry even more. Through her tears, she said, "I'm so sorry. Please forgive me, Mr. and Mrs. B. Oh god, please forgive me!"

Stacey's parents came to apologize to us, and we told them and Stacey that we forgive her and that we still love her. Stacey's mom said that we all needed to heal, and that would take some time. Her dad told us how sorry they were and asked for our forgiveness. He said he wanted for us to still be friends and hoped we could be. Hank told him that we could and that God would guide us through this. The fathers shook hands and then embraced. So did

Stacey's mom and I. Then the detectives took us to meet the young man who came forward.

"Mr. and Mrs. Baxter, this is Curtis Shelby," Detective Sweeney said.

"Hello, Curtis," Hank said as he shook his hand. "It is an honor to meet you. We can't thank you enough for coming forward with the truth. What made you do it?"

Curtis answered, "Hello, Mr. and Mrs. Baxter. I remember hearing about Jan last year when it happened. I remembered her face from the picture on the news and how they said she was such a nice, caring, and funny person. They said everyone liked her. How could I not speak up for someone like her? She sounded like the type of person that would be a good friend to anyone. She didn't deserve what happened to her. I felt sick when Carla told me what she did. I didn't want anything to do with her and couldn't believe I knew such a person. I had to tell the police. I believe Jan would have done it for me if it were the other way around."

"Yes, she would have, Curtis," I interjected. "She was raised to do the right thing and love all people no matter what others thought. Thank you for helping to fight for her. I can't help wondering what her last moments where like when she knew what was about to happen to her," I said softly.

"I can tell you that!" Curtis said. "Carla said when she showed Jan the gun and told her to walk into the woods, Jan started talking to her about becoming a Christian. Carla said she couldn't stand it and told her to be quiet. She said she only wanted to scare Jan. Once in the woods, she told Carla she needed to give her life to God and live for him. Then she said Jan said something strange."

"What?" I asked. He continued, "She said just before she pulled the trigger, Jan told her she loved her and she hoped that she would see her in heaven someday. She also said that if one of them had to go, she was glad it was her because she was ready and told Carla she wasn't."

I put my hand up to my mouth. "Oh my god, Hank, did you hear that? I'm so proud of Jan. I've never been more proud to be her mother." Hank put his arm around me and said, "Me too, honey. I guess we raised her right. Thank you, Curtis, for telling us that. You'll never know what that means to us, and on behalf of our other children, thank you." Curtis told us that Carla said she had been having nightmares about the whole thing. She also said that those words Jan told her at the end haunt her. "God bless you, Curtis," Hank said as he shook his hand. I hugged Curtis and prayed for him silently while he was in my arms.

Detective Sweeney asked us if we wanted to see Carla. Hank and I looked at each other. He grabbed my hand and asked if I were up to it. I took a deep breath and said, "We have to finish what Jan started, honey." Hank knew exactly what I meant. We asked the detective to give us a few moments to gather our thoughts. We went to sit in the cafeteria.

"How do you feel, honey? Are you angry at Carla?" Hank asked.

"Well, yes, I am! But mostly I'm relieved that this is finally at an end. It has been almost a year, and it's time for us all to move on. I just don't understand why people feel they can just take another person's life. Don't they stop and think that this person has a future?"

Hank replied, "No, they don't, Martha. They think very selfishly. That's why they commit such crimes. Jealousy is a very dangerous thing if not dealt with properly." Then I asked Hank how he felt. "I'm angry at Carla, yes, but also at the force behind what she did. She was driven silently by jealousy and rage to do what she did. Then she came to our house and sat in our daughter's room the day of the funeral like nothing had happened. I think if we had known at the time, Justin would have killed Carla and Stacey. And Jeff, I don't know what he would have done. I wish we had our Jan back, but if she had to go, I'm glad she went witnessing for God. Honey, do you really realize what Jan did?" I told Hank that I did realize what she did. She did the same thing Jesus did when he died on the cross. She forgave Carla for what she was about to do to her. Suddenly, Hank said, "Yeah, baby, you're right. We have to finish what Jan started. We must forgive." Hank prayed softly and asked God to help us forgive Carla.

We told Detective Sweeney we were now ready. Detective Swift came with us. I couldn't believe my eyes when I saw Carla. She was in handcuffs and had on what looked like orange scrubs, but mostly she looked so old and tired. She had dark circles under her eyes, which were puffy. Her nose was deep red. Her hair was a mess. As we got closer to her, I could see strands of gray mixed with her auburn hair. There was a thick glass between us as we sat on one side and she sat on the other. A female guard stood close by her. She would not look at us.

I said, "Carla? Is that you?" She would not reply. Just then, she wiped her nose with the tissue she held in her hand. Her hair covered her face. I didn't know what to say to her. I felt frozen and speechless. Hank reached for my hand.

"Carla," Hank said softly, "will you talk to us please?" She would not respond.

"Let's go, Hank," I said. As we were leaving, Carla called out to us.

We turned, and for the first time, she was looking at us. We went back to sit down. We could not believe we were looking at an eighteen-year-old girl. This looked like an old woman. "Mrs. B, Mr. B, I'm sorry," Carla said softly as she held her head down. "So many times I wished I could go back to that day. I didn't mean to pull the trigger. I just wanted to scare her. I didn't know what to do 'cause I was scared and had just turned eighteen. Stacey just stood there. I guess she was in shock. The only thing I could think of was to make it look like she did it herself. So I got the other gun I had and put it in Jan's hand and then pulled the trigger with her finger. I guess I got that from watching different movies. I'm so sorry for the pain I caused you and your family and everyone else. Now Jeff, the one I was trying to get, as well as everyone, hates me. But I don't blame them. I hate myself. I wish I could die. The crazy part about that is that I'm actually scared to die."

Hank asked, "Why are you scared to die, Carla?"

She continued, "I've been having dreams since all this happened. I keep seeing monsters dancing all around Jan while she is standing there, telling me about my life and how I need to live for God. The monsters keep saying, 'Kill her, kill her, kill her.' Every time they reach out to try to touch her, they get shocked by some invisible shield around her. And when I pulled the trigger, the bullet bounces off and gets me. As I lay there bleeding, the monsters laugh and say to me, 'You are so stupid.' Then they start eating me while I'm lying there dying. Then I could hear Jan say, 'Don't die yet, Carla, you're not ready, but I am.' I'm even scared to go to sleep sometimes."

Hank and I looked at each other. Then between the two of us, we explained to Carla about being a Christian and living right. We told her how Jesus died on the cross for us all.

She said, "Even me?"

We told her yes. After we finished explaining to her what Jan meant, for the first time since we were sitting there, we saw some hope in her eyes. My heart melted after I'd heard all she had been through. I asked the detectives if I could touch Carla. They said I was not allowed to, but under the circumstances, they would allow it. Hank and I went in to where she was, and with her still in handcuffs, I hugged her as she cried. Hank came and gently held her too. I never thought I would see the day when we would be embracing our daughter's killer. Never! By doing this, I knew Carla needed this more than we did. Hank told Carla how she could become born again and live a new life and have the old one forgiven and forgotten by God.

"Is that possible?" she asked.

"Yes," I said. "When Jesus forgave the ones responsible for his death, God forgave them too. Jan forgave you, Carla, and now God wants to forgive you."

It was as if I were standing outside of my body, watching and listening to what was going on. We were about to lead our daughter's killer to Christ. I couldn't stop it, and I didn't want to stop it. But was this fair? Was this right? It didn't matter. I just wanted to see this poor young girl free from her own prison. As detectives Swift and Sweeney stood by along with the guard, Hank and I led Carla to her new life in Christ. Hank asked the detectives to remove the cuffs for a moment. They hesitated but removed them. Carla threw her arms around us and began to cry tears of joy.

"Now I know I am ready to die. Mr. and Mrs. B, I'm sure you are proud of your daughter. I wish I had parents like you. If I had, I wouldn't have done what I did. You guys are good role models."

"Carla, we have to put the cuffs back on," Detective Swift said.

"Yes, sir, and thank you," Carla responded. Then something strange happened. Carla smiled. "I haven't done that in so long," she said. "But now I feel like I've got a reason to smile. I didn't ever think you guys would forgive me. So many people say they are Christians and don't live like it. You don't just say you're Christians. You live what you say."

As we were leaving, Carla called out to us, and we turned around. "Thank you, Mr. and Mrs. B."

I walked over to her and kissed her forehead and said, "You're welcome, Carla." Tears streamed down her face, and I wiped them away.

When we got home, we told Justin and Jessica everything that happened. There were mixed emotions from them both. Justin wanted to go to the police station to see Stacey and Carla. He also wanted to meet Curtis and thank him personally. Hank didn't like the look in Justin's eyes.

"Justin, why do you want to see Carla and Stacey?" Hank asked.

"So I can tell them I'm glad they're in prison and even that's too good for them. They need to die in the electric chair, and I want to be there to watch."

"Dad, what's going to happen to Carla and Stacey?" Jess asked.

"The detectives said Carla will be tried as an adult since she was eighteen when she committed the crime, and Stacey will have to serve some time for withholding evidence."

"I hope both of them fry," Justin said.

"Justin, Stacey didn't know what Carla was going to do, so you shouldn't be so mad at her. Maybe a little, but she didn't kill our sister. Carla did," Jess said.

"I don't care," Justin said as he walked out of the room.

"He'll be fine," Hank said. "God is working on him even though we can't see it."

Three Years Later

Today is Carla's execution for the death of our daughter Jan Margaret Baxter. Each one of us has been to visit Carla, except Justin. Jess has been able to talk to her and make peace with her. Both Jess and Justin have been to see Stacey and made peace with her. We have been invited to the execution, and at Carla's request, we will be there. Hank gave Carla a Bible three years ago, and once a week, we went to have Bible study with her and a group of other inmates. While we were waiting for the execution to take place, we spoke to Carla's mother who raised her and her two brothers on her own. She was so grateful to us for spending time with her daughter and for forgiving her. She didn't know that Justin was angry with her daughter, and at the execution, she told Justin that Carla said that if it were not for Jan, she would never have come to know God.

"What do you mean?" Justin wanted to know.

She told him how Jan witnessed to her about Jesus and told her that if one of them had to die, she was glad it was her and not Carla because Carla wasn't ready. She told him Carla didn't know what she meant at the time, but his parents explained it to her. She further told him of the dreams her daughter had before her new life in Christ. Carla's mom told Justin that Jan forgave Carla for killing her before she did it, and as a result of Jan's courage, Carla got a new life in Christ, and she did too. She also told Justin that her sons were next.

Hearing all these things from Carla's mom and seeing the tears in her eyes made Justin realize that his sister died for a cause. He suddenly realized that she died with purpose. Through her death, two souls came to Jesus, and two more would come as a result, as well as all the ones they would win to God before it was all over. He came to understand that through his sister's death, many would come to know God. He now understood what his parents said three years ago the day they came home from the police station. Suddenly, Justin's baby sister became his hero. He no longer felt anger toward Carla or God. He understood.

Now Carla was ready for her execution. She was asked if there was anything she wanted to say. "Yes, I would like to say how sorry I am for what I did. Jan was truly a beautiful person, and if it weren't for her, I wouldn't be on my way home now. Mom, stay close to the Baxter family. They will help you to continue to grow in God. Kiss Kevin and Lester for me and tell them to be good and don't do anything bad. Prison life is not for anyone. I love you, Mom! Mr. B, thank you for the Bible you gave me. Please give it to my mom. There is a letter in it for you, Mom, from me. To the Baxter family, thanks for my life. I know that sounds ironic, but you know what I mean. I love you all. To everyone else, try God . . . Life with him is worth living. I'm ready to go home now."

There was a moment of silence.

Then Justin called to Carla, "I forgive you, Carla, for what you did to my sister." Carla smiled at Justin and said thank you. The order was given to start the execution.

As Carla was dying, Jessica shouted out, "Tell Jan hello and we love her." Carla looked at us, smiled weakly, gave a thumbs-up, and winked her eye.

I will not tell anyone that forgiveness is easy because sometimes it is not. Sometimes it takes time to let go and start over. God is our refuge and strength, a very present help in trouble. Time is a healer (Psalm 46:1). One thing we all learned from this whole experience is that the saying is true, "A family that prays together, stays together." We all miss Jan and Carla too.

I am happy to say that Carla's mom has grown tremendously in Christ, and one of her brothers is a Christian too. It is unfortunate that her other brother is very bitter about what happened to his sister and doesn't want anything to do with God—*yet*. Stacey is out of prison and doing well. Jeff continues to go to church with us and is like a son to us. Things don't always turn out like we want, but we learn as we go on.

I appreciate my husband so much because he showed himself to be the strong man of God he is. Justin admires him and aspires to be like him. Hank helped to keep us together with his wisdom and leads us through Bible readings and prayer. He really is the head of our family, and I love him.

Jessica is doing well and is engaged to be married in the spring. We all love her fiancé. Justin changed his major in college and is studying law now. He wants to be a judge someday to help society God's way. I am doing well and volunteer through the police department to help families that have lost a loved one through tragedy. Hank and I have Bible studies once a month to help them. We usually have a good turnout. For all these, we say, "To God be the glory."

The Stranger Called Daddy

And ye fathers provoke not your children to wrath: but bring them up in the nurture and admonition of the Lord.
Ephesians 6:4

I remember Daddy picking me up and tossing me into the air, both of us laughing and giggling. He seemed like the bravest man in the whole world. He always seemed to know what to do and what to say. My daddy was my hero. He could do no wrong in my eyes. He was the smartest man alive. That was my daddy. I had the best dad anyone could ever want. He seemed so big. I remember looking up into his face. Surely my father was at least ten feet tall. At least to me he was. He stood out in any crowd. I remember his laughter and smile. He had dimples so deep I thought they were holes in his cheeks. I would stick my little fingers into them as he smiled. My daddy was so special to me. One day, I promised myself I would marry someone just like him. Then when I was four years old, he was gone. He didn't even say goodbye. Daddy tucked me in bed one night and kissed my forehead and disappeared until I was thirteen. Of course, there were some phone calls and promises made and not kept. Then the news came that he married someone I'd never met.

My mom sat down with me one Saturday morning and told me that my father called and wanted to see me. I thought, *Why?* But Mom raised me not to be selfish or self-centered. So I said okay. Mom prayed with me and asked God to have his way in the meeting. I thank God for my mother because she never spoke badly against my father. Whatever happened between them was between them. She never brought me into it. Instead, she would keep those happy memories of me and Daddy fresh in my mind.

So now at thirteen, my father wanted to see me again. I didn't know what to say to him or even what he would look like. The moment arrived when he rang the doorbell. Mom answered the door, and he came in. I stood there looking at him as if he were a stranger. Well, he was a stranger to me; after all, I hadn't seen him since I was four years old. He held out his arms to embrace me, so we embraced. It was so awkward. Then he spoke. As he did, I closed my eyes, and I heard Daddy again. The voice was the same. I smiled at the memory of Daddy's voice. We sat on the couch, and he asked all kinds of questions about me. It was like meeting a stranger for the first time. A familiar stranger. Then he told me that he had married again and wanted me to meet his new wife and that I had a baby sister. *Wow! I have a sister.* It has always been Mom and me. My mom is my mom, but she is also my friend. How would a sister and a stepmother fit into my world, not to mention my father? I asked my father how old my sister was. He said four.

Before I realized it, I blurted out, "That's how old I was when you left me!" At that point, I couldn't hold back the tears. *This is too much for me*, I thought. Mom came running into the room, and I ran into her arms. My father held his head down and didn't know what to say.

Just then, he managed to say softly, "Maybe this wasn't such a good idea."

Mom said, "Yes, maybe it would be better if you tried another time."

As my father was walking to the front door, I said, "No, don't go. I may never see you again. I want to meet my sister."

Mom asked me if I was sure I felt up to it. My father said he didn't want to cause me any more pain than he had already. I told them both that I was sure. I dried my eyes and hugged Mom and told her that for some reason, I felt peaceful. She looked at me, smiled, and said, "Jesus is with you." So I left with this stranger called Daddy.

The car ride to the hotel where my father and his new family were staying was so quiet. I had so many questions but didn't know how to ask them. The silence was broken by my father's voice, asking me if I wanted to stop and get something to eat. I said no.

He said, "How about ice cream?"

I sensed that he wanted to talk to me before I met his new family, so I said, "I guess so."

We stopped at the ice cream shop by the ocean. As we sat beside the water, eating our ice cream, my father said to me, "I'll bet you have so many questions you want to ask and don't know how to ask them. Am I right?"

"Yes," I said.

He said to me, "Can I ask you a question, baby girl?" I hadn't heard that since I was four. It made me happy and sad all at the same time hearing my father's voice saying that once again.

"Yes, you can ask me something, but don't call me baby girl. Call me by my name, Lisa."

"That's fair," he said. "Are you angry with me?" I told him I used to be, but now I have gotten used to his not being around. I am quite happy with it being just Mom and me. He asked if my mother ever explained why he left. I said no, she never spoke of it or spoke negatively against him in my presence. I told him I guess that was why I didn't really feel any bitterness toward him.

He held his head down and said, "Your mother was always a good woman. I didn't know how well until now. She has done a great job raising you."

He told me that when he was a boy, his father left them, and he didn't see him again until he was a grown man. He said, "My father didn't want anything to do with me or my brother." He continued by telling me that his parents fought all the time and his father drank a lot. Finally, his mother couldn't take the physical or verbal abuse anymore and neither could she take having to find new places to hide the rent money to keep him from drinking it up. One day, during a big fight between his father and mother, he and his brother came home from school to find their father choking the life out of their mother, whose face was swollen and turning blue. We jumped on our father and began beating him until he let our mother go. She fell to the floor, and he ran out of the house, never to return.

"That was the last time I saw my father until I was a grown man. My brother and I took good care of our mother until she died ten years ago when you were three. She loved you so much and played with you all the time. She was the one who started calling you baby girl. My mother was filled with bitterness against my father, and she always spoke badly about him.

"About a year after your mother and I were married, we began going to church. We felt that it would be good to raise our family in the church. Or should I say your mother felt that way. It didn't matter to me because I never saw much that God did for us coming up. Before long, your mother became a Christian. Whatever your mother did, she did it with passion. When you were born, you were my world, you and your mother, as long as she didn't talk that religious stuff to me. I used to take you to the stables to look at the horses, to the zoo, pet stores, parks, everywhere. And we always had fun.

"Then one day, I came home from work to find my mother

at our house with your mother. Mother was crying. As I hurried to my mother's side, I asked what happened as memories of my father making her cry flooded my mind. My eyebrows met in the middle. My mother reached up and began to stroke the side of my face and said, 'Relax those worrying lines on your forehead. I'm not sad. I'm happy. You see tears of joy.' At that moment, I took Mother's hand and kissed it, feeling relief. She continued, 'You are my precious Walter, my firstborn. You are the gentlest man I know but full of such bitterness and hatred toward your father. I know because I helped to feed that to you over the years. Son, I was wrong. Today, for the first time in many, many years, I've finally found the love and peace I had been longing for. Son, I asked Jesus to forgive me of all my sins and come live in my heart and take away all the pain and bitterness of yesterday. I told him I want the rest of my days on earth to be filled with his joy.' Just then, she reached both hands out and held my face. 'Walter,' she said, 'I've never known joy or love like this before. There is a peace that I can't explain, but I can say, though I remember the past, I forgive all wrong done to me, and I forgive myself for all the wrong I've done to others. I couldn't do that for all these years. Only since I asked Jesus into my heart was I able to do it. It's because of him that I have this freedom in my mind and heart.' I saw a different mother from that day until she died. She began going to church with your mother and never missed going until she went home to be with the Lord."

Just then, he reached into his jacket pocket and took out an envelope and gave it to me. He said, "Many years ago, your grandmother made me promise to give this to you when you were old enough to understand."

As I held it, thoughts were flooding my mind of the story I was just told. "Wow" is all I could muster up to say.

Then I asked my father if he knew what was in the envelope. He said, "No, I promised Mother that it wouldn't be opened until you opened it." Then he looked down and said, "That is one promise I kept.

"Lisa, I want you to know that I've made many mistakes in my life, and the one I regret the most is not being in your life. I can't go back and change any of the past, but I learned that the future is so full of possibilities. Lisa, will you forgive me for leaving you and your mother? I was a wimp and couldn't handle her new lifestyle. I guess I felt so convicted and couldn't handle it. I ran like my father. Then I felt ashamed to come back. You see we were always taught that parents never apologize to their children. Children were seen and not heard. We had no opinion. Well, in recent months, I've learned that it is a deception to believe that parents should not apologize to their children because wrong is wrong no matter who does it. I also learned that parents are supposed to be examples to their children. If we want our children to be good parents, we must show them how to deal with wrong even when we do it. When my mother apologized to me, my heart began to melt. A bond greater than we had ever had before began to develop between us. I didn't totally understand Mother's new lifestyle, but I admired her more than words could ever say."

Many things went through my mind. Old memories, new ones being created, my grandmother, my grandfather, and my mother. I wondered what my mother would do if she were me. As I looked at my father waiting patiently for my response, all I could say was "Have you forgiven *your* father?"

Then my father said, "Wait one minute." He walked a little ways away and made a call on his cell phone. When he came back, he said, "Yes, Lisa, I have forgiven my father. You see one day, I was so broken, I decided to walk. I considered killing myself. As I walked, I met a man who saw my pain. He told me I looked like he did three years prior. As he spoke, I heard hope in his voice. I asked him how he got through his pain. He told me there is only one way to rid yourself of it permanently, and that is by asking

God to forgive you of all your sins and asking him to come into your heart and live through you. He said after that you live one day at a time, and soon you will come to realize you aren't hurting as bad as before, and gradually, he replaces that pain with love. His love. The man told me all my answers were in Jesus, and if I gave him a try, he would not let me down. I was desperate. It was either Jesus or killing myself. I had no hope, no dreams, no peace, and no more strength. I remembered what I saw in Mother's eyes after she accepted Jesus into her heart. I remembered your mother and her passion for Christ. They both were better people for their decision, and now this gentleman was telling me the same thing happened to him. What would it hurt to try? So right on that sidewalk in the park, I got on my knees and asked the Lord to forgive me of all my many sins and mistakes. At that moment, I saw your precious face as I kissed your forehead before I left you and your mother. I asked him to come into my heart and live through me. All of a sudden, I felt as if the world was lifted off my shoulders. That's all. Nothing around me changed. My hands looked the same, and my clothes were too. Even the gentleman looked the same. But how could that be? I knew something was different. Then the man looked at me, smiled, and said, 'What you feel is the peace of God that you cannot explain.' Somehow, the hate I felt toward my father changed to pity. What was happening to me? I began to weep uncontrollably. But these tears were making me feel wonderful. The man embraced me and held me tight. I hadn't felt another man embrace me like that ever. My brother and I embrace, but nothing like that."

Just then, a car drove up to where we were. My father said, "This is my wife and daughter."

They got out of the car, and the little girl ran to my father, shouting, "Daddy!"

He said, "Alyssa, this is your big sister, Lisa." She had an amazing resemblance to my father.

She smiled and said, "Hi, Lisa." She had deep dimples that looked like holes in her cheeks like my father.

I said, "Hi, Alyssa."

Just then, she reached out to hug me and said, "I love you, Lisa." I smiled, and then to my surprise, she reached her hands to my face and put her fingers in my cheeks and said, "You got holes like me and Daddy." I laughed and cried at the same time.

Then my father said, "Lisa, I want you to meet my wife, Peggy." She seemed nervous to meet me.

I embraced her and said, "Hello."

My father said, "She is a Christian too. We met at church." Just then, he waved to the car, and an old man got out and came over to us. "Lisa, this is my father, Paul. It turns out that he is also the man who led me to Christ."

"What? How? What?" That is all I could say.

As tears welled up in my grandfather's eyes, he smiled and said, "Hello, Lisa. It is an honor to meet you. You look just like your grandmother."

At that moment, I noticed my grandfather had holes in his cheeks too. "Oh, my grandmother," I said. I had forgotten about the envelope my father gave me. I picked it up off the rock I had been sitting on. "Excuse me please," I said as I turned and walked a few feet away.

I opened the envelope and pulled out a picture wrapped in beautiful ivory lace stationary. On the stationary were these words:

> My dearest baby girl,
>
> I don't know what events have shaped your life, but I feel compelled to tell you how much I love you and that Jesus loves you too. We all make mistakes in our lives, and one of the hardest things to do is to forgive. But with forgiveness comes great rewards. I used to have unforgiveness in my heart, but because

of the forgiveness of God, I was able to forgive and let the past go. Always remember, forgiveness leads to peace.

Love,
Your grandmother, Lisa

On the picture was my grandmother holding me and my father sitting next to her, smiling. I could not control the tears, and my father ran to me and took me in his arms and held me tight. I broke down even more. Just then, I felt Alyssa hugging my legs, and Peggy came and embraced me too. I felt so much love. Then I opened my eyes and saw my grandfather wiping his eyes with a handkerchief.

I broke the embrace and walked over to him and said, "You need to read this." I gave him the letter my grandmother wrote me.

As he read it, he broke down uncontrollably too. Then he said, "Now I know that she forgave me."

I looked at my father and said, "Daddy, I want to ask Jesus to forgive me too." My father led me to the Lord right there on the oceanfront in the presence of my grandfather, sister, stepmother, and mother. I didn't realize that when my father made that phone call, he called Peggy to come to where we were and bring everyone with her and to call my mother and tell her to come too. Somehow, it seemed as if my grandmother was there as well. I was so happy to see my mom and that she was there to share that moment with me. It all seemed so overwhelming.

My grandfather lived an additional six years. He shared with me that God had healed him from a damaged liver because of all the drinking he did in earlier years. He also told me how beautiful my grandmother was. My mother shared with me many things about my grandmother, including how she led her to the Lord and watched her life and attitude change.

So now the stranger called Daddy is no longer a stranger. He has become one of my best friends. He spends a lot of time sharing the Bible with me and Alyssa, helping us to grow up in the Lord. I was so blessed watching his father do the same with him. My grandfather moved in with my father and Peggy. They all moved to the same city where we live because my father wanted to be a part of my life. Now every Father's Day, I make a special effort no matter what to spend it with my father.

At my grandfather's funeral, my father and my uncle told of how Granddad led them to Christ. They learned how to forgive from their mother *and* father. What seemed like destined for failure God turned around and got great glory out of it.

Fathering a baby doesn't make you a daddy. Nurturing, loving, being there, and speaking into your children's lives identify a *daddy*. There are many fathers out there, but where are the *daddies*? No matter what happened in the past or what did not happen, let it go. Seek out your children and make the most of the future. Look ahead, not behind, Daddy.

Double Whammy

> Finally, my brethren, be strong in the Lord, and in the
> power of his might. Put on the whole armor of God that
> ye may be able to stand against the wiles of the devil.
> Ephesians 6:10–11

First of all, let me tell you a little something about myself. My name is Sherri

Williamson. My life growing up was hard. I had eight sisters and three brothers and often got lost in the crowd. At times, I felt my parents didn't know I existed. I was the third from the youngest of twelve. I was not particularly close to my brothers and was tolerated by my sisters.

My oldest sister, Brenda, looked out for me. It seemed more like she was my mother rather than my sister. By the time my two youngest sisters and I came along, my parents were tired of children and relied on the older siblings to raise the younger ones.

My father was gone all the time, and my mother was always stressed by problems she was having with my father and his mistresses. Needless to say, I could do pretty much whatever I wanted when I was away from home. I loved school because there I mattered. Math was my favorite subject, and it seemed I was always winning an award for some reason. My teachers said it was because of my math skills, but to me, I was just doing something I enjoyed.

We lived by the ocean, so when I was at home and not doing chores, I was down by the water counting something, anything. The ocean was my place of tranquility. There was always someone fighting at home, but at the ocean, I was in control. My dog and I wandered and made many discoveries together. Every day by the ocean was a new adventure for me. We found and buried treasures and set traps for anyone trying to steal them. We even rescued people off deserted islands. Even if it was the same old thing, in my mind, I made it something new. I always found a way to make an equation and solve it.

By the time I was thirteen, I found out I was not a bad-looking girl, and my body was changing. I wasn't the only one making that discovery. The boys were noticing too. Leroy, a boy in my class, began to like me and did so off and on for the next ten years. But then I guess it's true; you never forget your first. Slowly, Leroy began to replace the ocean in my life. I began spending a lot of time with him. At the age of fourteen, we explored sexual intimacy and decided we loved it. I thought that because I had sex with Leroy, I had to marry him when we were old enough. Leroy thought that because he had sex with me, he was now obligated to share this experience with all the pretty girls he met. Thus began our off-and-on relationship.

When I was fifteen, something totally unexpected happened to me; I got pregnant. I didn't understand the changes happening to me and was scared. My mother never explained to me about girls having menstrual cycles; it just happened to me. I thought I was dying or something until my sister Brenda explained to me what was happening and showed me how to take care of myself and use feminine products. Now once again, Brenda came to my rescue. Most girls probably tell their mothers first that they're pregnant, but not me. I told Brenda first. Brenda was married and had a son of her own by then, so I spent a lot of time at her house babysitting for her and her husband. I loved my sister so much and thanked God for her many times. She came with me when I told my mother. I'll never forget what my mother said, "Oh well, just don't do it again." That's it, nothing else. I was so scared and told her, but that was all she said.

When I told Leroy, he was angry and said he wasn't ready to be a father. I felt hurt and unwanted. I couldn't explain the feelings that were going on inside of me; I wished I didn't exist. When Leroy's mother found out I was pregnant with his child, she was loving toward me and made me feel some sense of worth.

Things at home got harder. My father wouldn't much look at me anymore because I was pregnant. He gave me extra chores to do and made me eat disgusting concoctions, saying it was good for the baby. His version of a vegetable medley, kidney and beef cakes, and a drink made with milk and something green, which tasted awful. Now that I look back on it, I guess it was his way of taking care of me and the baby. At that time, I just thought he hated me and was being mean. My mother didn't say much to me or encourage me on how to take care of myself. But then again, she was going through so much herself with my father. She was tired of children anyway and said it was just another mouth to feed. I felt no love at home, so I asked my sister Brenda if I could move in with her and her family. She said yes, and I left home and didn't look back. Mother was glad because she didn't know what to do with me anyway since I disappointed and embarrassed her.

When I had my baby, it was a boy. I was scared and alone. Leroy didn't come around much until he heard he had a son. At that time, he wanted to play the role of proud papa. He came to the hospital with his chest stuck out and insisted on his son being named Leroy Jr. I didn't have the strength to fight with him; besides, maybe he had a change of heart and was now ready to be with me and his son. My parents didn't even come to the hospital, but they came to see the baby and me after we were home from the hospital. My mother smiled when she saw the baby, held him, and asked how I was doing. That made me feel as if my mother really did care about me and my son. She told me before they left that she really did love me and that she wanted to be a better grandmother to my child than she was a mother to me. My father looked at my son and said, "Thank God it's a boy. Girls only bring babies and trouble." It hurt to hear my father say that because I knew he was talking about me.

I was not ready for what life held for me next. My son screaming through the night and keeping me up, and I had to go to school and work the next day. Day in and day out, it was the same. My friends were out partying, having fun, and here I was playing house. It wasn't fair. Leroy wasn't going through this, so why should I? I asked my parents if they would take my son and raise him for a while until I finished high school and saved enough money to get my own apartment. Before I could get it all out, my father shouted, "Hell no! You got yourself into this. Now you deal with it." Brenda and her husband couldn't do it either because Brenda was now expecting her second child. The only other thing I could think of was to ask Leroy. "Are you crazy?" he asked. But the next day at school, he told me that his mother said she would take Leroy Jr. for a while. *A while* turned out to be forever. I spent much time with Leroy Jr., making sure he knew I was his mother.

Now this was more like it. I could now go out with my friends and be a teenager. Leroy and I picked up where we left off. We partied, danced, and got drunk. Looking back on all these, I can't believe I called that fun.

One night, my girlfriend and I went to a club and met some guys from another country. They had nice accents and were fine, so we hung out with them for a while. This was during one of my off times with Leroy. However, when he found out about it, he was angry. He came to my house the next night at 11:00 p.m. He was drunk and banging on the door, telling me to come out so he could talk to me. My brother-in-law went out to tell him to go home and not to come to his house at that hour again drunk. He told him he wasn't leaving until he spoke to me. So I went out and told my brother-in-law it was all right, and he went back inside. While I was talking to Leroy, he got very angry and slapped me for hanging out with those foreign guys. That shocked me because he had never done that before, and before I knew it, I slapped him back. One thing led to another, and my brother-in-law had to come back out to break us up from fighting. As Leroy was leaving, he shouted to me, "I love you, Sherri."

I know it sounds strange, but that was our relationship. Love, fight, breakup, makeup, sex. A few times in between, I got pregnant and had abortions. I knew it was wrong, but I couldn't go through the screaming baby stage again.

When I was twenty-one, I got pregnant again by Leroy. This time, I had learned more about life and decided not to have an abortion. I had graduated from high school and was making my way through college. I was working and paying for my classes at the community college. I only had another three months to go, and then I would graduate from college. At least this time when I would have the baby, I would be a college graduate with a degree in business management. Leroy and I were not doing really well. He was seeing other girls, and I was tired of fighting with him about it. I decided to let him go for good and move on with my life. It was unfortunate because now we were going to have another child, but I was stable now and more focused. By this time, Leroy had two other children and wasn't interested in another.

The day I graduated from college was the day I found out I was having twins. Talk about a double whammy! I never even thought about that possibility. As I sat in the tub, getting my bath, I was in deep thought. When I had Leroy Jr., it was hard for me, so now his grandmother was raising him. What was I going to do with twins? Two screaming babies keeping me up at night! How was I going to do it? I lived alone and had broken up with Leroy. Going back home was not an option, and Brenda had a full house now. I made up my mind that I was having my babies, and we were going to survive and thrive. So that evening, when I walked across that stage, pregnant with my twins, to get my diploma, it was a new beginning for us and a momentous moment. I shared this auspicious occasion with my twins; this was the first of many.

Once I graduated, I landed a job working as a personal banker at Bank of Briggs Brothers, to which I was excelling fast. Now I could put all those number skills to practice and make good money from it. And that I was. I was receiving excellent paychecks and saving all I could. I knew having one baby was expensive, so two had to be twice as expensive. I rarely heard from Leroy, and when he did come around, he only wanted one thing—sex. I didn't really know what was happening to me, but I didn't want that lifestyle anymore. I told him that I respected myself and my unborn children and that I would not be having sex again until it was with my husband. He laughed, of course, and said, "And how long do you think that will last? You know you'll be calling me for this," pointing to himself. Happily, I can say he never got that call.

One day while I was at work, my girlfriend Krystal and I went to the Cajun Lobster for lunch. Our department had won the most sales, so they gave us an extended lunch hour. While we were there, two very distinguished gentlemen came into the restaurant for lunch. Krystal had caught the eye of one.

"Look, Sherri, that guy is so handsome, and he keeps looking at me."

I laughed and asked her what she would do if he decided to come over and say something to her. As we were laughing about it, both gentlemen came over. We were speechless.

"Hello, ladies, my colleague and I were wondering if you ladies would mind if we come over and meet you."

Krystal said, "Oh, that's fine."

Here I was, big and pregnant, feeling a bit left out, but why not go along with the fun? After all, it was an opportunity for Krystal to meet someone.

The men sat down at our table and introduced themselves to us. "My name is Brian, and this is my colleague, Brandon."

Brandon extended his hand out to me and shook my hand gently. "Hello, ladies, I hope we are not intruding on your lunch. We just wanted to meet you."

I was flattered. We sat and talked and ended up having lunch together. Krystal and Brian seemed to get along great. Brandon was so sweet to me. When it was time for us to go back to work, Brandon asked me if he could see me again.

My eyes were probably as big as quarters. I replied, "Why would you want to see me again? Don't you see that I'm pregnant?"

"Yes, of course, I see that," he said, laughing. "You seem to be a very nice young lady, and I would like to get to know you better. Is there anything wrong with that? You said you are single and unattached, and I understand that things happen."

Krystal looked at me, smiling.

"All right," I said, "but I'm not looking for any sort of attachment."

Three months later, I gave birth to beautiful twin girls, and Brandon was right by my side in the birthing room. So much for attachments. Not only were we attached, but also he told me he had fallen in love with me and wanted to spend the rest of his life with me raising the girls together. The day after I gave birth, Leroy came by the hospital once again with his chest stuck out. He was passing out pink bubblegum cigars. I hadn't seen him in almost four months. He told me he wanted to get back together, but I told him he was just caught up in the moment. I explained that I had someone else in my life, and he laughed and asked who would want a woman who had just given birth to twins.

All of a sudden, these words filled the room: "I would, and I do want this woman. I love her and accept her children too."

I turned to the door, and there was Brandon standing in the doorway, holding the most beautiful flowers I had ever seen and two pink stuffed teddy bears.

Leroy said, "Man, who are you?"

Brandon came in and kissed me on the forehead and gave me the flowers and put the stuffed teddy bears on the table next to the bed, along with the other flowers he had sent to the hospital. He extended his hand to Leroy, and they shook hands. Then Brandon introduced himself. After an awkward moment with these two men, Leroy asked Brandon to give us a few minutes so he could talk to me.

"So, Sherri, I see you got yourself a good guy. He seems to be all right, and I guess he really likes you, huh? Just don't forget, *I'm those girls' father!*"

When he was finished staking his claim, I asked him, "What are *those girls'* names?"

He paused, looked at me, and said, "I don't know. Did you name them yet?"

I replied, "Yes, I did name them. It took a lot of patience for me to get through college and this pregnancy, and God has granted me his grace to endure all that I have and come out on top. Their names are Patience and Grace."

Leroy shook his head up and down in acceptance and said, "You've been through a lot, Sherri. Okay, you deserve all the good coming your way." Leroy leaned down and kissed me on the cheek and whispered in my ear, "I'm glad you're the mother of my children. Well, at least three of them."

We both laughed, and then he went to the nursery to see the girls.

Brandon came back in and asked me if I was all right.

"Yeah, Brandon, I'm fine. Thank you for asking. You're quite a gentleman."

He came and sat on the side of the bed and said, "Sherri, I have grown to love you so much. You are a strong woman with will and determination. You are a fighter with a gentle spirit. One day, I'm going to ask you to be my wife." Then he went over and got the stuffed teddy bears he had brought in earlier and gave them to me. Each of them had a small gold chain around their neck. Engraved on them were the girls' names.

I looked at Brandon and said, "You're so thoughtful."

As time went by, the girls grew, and Leroy came around from time to time, but Brandon was always there. When the girls were two years old, Brandon asked me to marry him, and I said yes. Brandon and Leroy weren't the best of friends, but they weren't enemies either. They spoke and tolerated each other. By now, I had moved up the ladder at work and was doing very well in my career. Brandon worked in politics and made a very lucrative salary. We bought a house by the ocean, and the girls learned to love nature like I did as a child.

One evening, Brandon came home excited about something that happened that day. He had a hard time waiting to tell me about it. After the girls were in bed, he said, "Honey, now can I share something with you?"

"Sure, Brandon, what is it?"

I was shocked when he said, "I got saved today." He seemed so happy, happier than I had ever seen him. He showed me the new Bible he bought earlier that day and gave me one too. "I want us to start going to church and bring the children up God's way." I was pleasantly surprised and wanted to know more about his experience. He told me Brian and Krystal had become Christians and shared their experience with him, and he asked Jesus to live in his heart too. Brian and Krystal had gotten married seven months before we did. They invited us to come to a Bible study at their house on that Friday. It was at that Bible study that I too gave my heart to the Lord.

Now we were on our way as a Christian family. We had our share of problems just like other families, but when we did, we went to the Bible to see what it said. Brandon and Brian were faithful men, and that was how they both climbed the ladder in their careers. They were just as faithful at church. The pastor noticed, and there they got promoted too. Brandon came to me one day and told me he felt God wanted him to go into the ministry and start his own church. I advised him to talk to the pastor about it. The pastor told Brandon God had already placed in his heart to start training him for pastoral ministry. Thus, it began. Lessons, hard ones too. Wow, I didn't know if I wanted to go through all these. But it never failed; with every hard lesson came great reward. Three years later, we were sent out to pastor our own church, with a few members to start. Brian and Krystal came with us. By then, they had two children of their own.

The girls were growing nicely and were active in school events. Patience was like her name, a very patient person with a gentle spirit. She loved art and animals, horses in particular. Grace was impetuous, quick, and sharp. She was very good with numbers and loved to read. It was nothing to find Grace curled up at night in bed with a flashlight and her book when she was supposed to be asleep. I had many challenges that came with being a wife, mother, pastor's wife, and banker. I always turned to the Bible for peace and consolation. Brandon and I had some serious challenges, but we got through them.

My children meant everything to me. Leroy Jr. came and spent some weekends with us. The girls loved having a big brother, and he loved being big brother. He proved to be quite protective of his sisters. He and Brandon didn't always get along, but somehow, it all worked out in the end. Every Sunday evening, we all sat around in the family room and had discussions about whatever the children wanted to talk about. This always proved interesting and kept the door open between the children and us.

Soon Leroy Jr. was off to college. I was so proud of my son. Watching him walk across that stage to get his high school diploma and knowing he would be off to college in the fall was a wonderful feeling. This time, I was the one with my chest stuck out. After his graduation, we all met at his grandmother's house where he lived. While there, I saw Leroy. I was sitting out on the patio, relaxing and pondering my son's life and future, when Leroy came out on the patio.

"May I join you, Sherri?" he asked.

"Sure," I said with a smile.

"So, Sherri, how have you been? I haven't seen you in a while. You're still one beautiful lady."

I blushed at the compliment and said thank you. "I'm doing great, Leroy. Thanks for asking. God has truly blessed me in spite of the rough places. What have you been doing with your life?" I asked.

Leroy responded, "I've been missing you, Sherri. We sure had some good times together. We should have stayed together and raised our children together. It was a mistake to let you go. How is Brandon treating you?" I wasn't expecting to hear what Leroy said. I was totally surprised by his comments. I guess the look on my face revealed that because he asked, "Why do you look so surprised?"

"It has been so long since we've seen each other, Leroy. You're quite the bachelor these days. I just never even considered you feeling like this after all these years."

"Sherri, I think about you all the time. I look for you in every woman that I meet and discovered that there is only one you."

"That's right, Leroy, and I belong to Brandon. I love my husband and am happy being his wife. I'll always care about you, but in a different way. We have a past together, but Brandon is my present and my future."

Leroy replied, "So you still care about me?"

"Of course, I do. But it's not the same as it was back then. This is the kind that wants to see your soul saved from hell. I want you to experience happiness in Jesus, Leroy. He makes you complete. When you have him, you don't have to go around looking for another me or anyone else. Give your life to him and let him take care of the rest. You'll meet the woman he has for you."

"Okay, okay, okay, that's enough of that, Sherri. If I want a sermon, I'll go talk to your husband. What do you think about our son graduating and going off to college?"

At that point, I smiled and told Leroy how proud I was of our son. Leroy Jr. also loved numbers and was going to college to become an accountant. Both Leroy and I were smiling and glowing when Leroy Jr. came out to join us.

"What are you two all smiles about?"

Leroy and I both said at the same time, "You!"

We laughed, and Leroy went over to shake his son's hand and congratulate him on his success and told him that we both were so proud of him.

Leroy Jr. looked over at me, and I smiled warmly at him and nodded my head. Tears began to roll down his face as he said, "This is the first time I've had my mother and father to myself."

I walked over to them, and Leroy and I hugged our son at the same time.

It was a moment none of us would ever forget.

That night while we were getting ready for bed, Brandon told me he saw the whole episode on the patio. I looked at him and asked if he heard any of it. "Yeah, I did, Sherri. I heard most of it. I was glad to hear you tell Leroy that he was your past and I'm your present and future. Thank you, honey, that meant a lot to me. I was also happy for Leroy Jr. I saw how important it was to him to have his mother and father together at that moment, that was why I didn't come out there. You all needed your time together."

I couldn't believe what I was hearing. I looked at my husband and ran over to him and gave him the biggest hug and almost squeezed the breath out of him. This is part of the reason I love my husband so much; he is very understanding. As I was hugging him, I whispered in his ear, "I'm so glad you are my husband. I'm blessed to be your wife."

Our church was doing well. We had many members and an active evangelism team. We visited prisons, hospitals, parks, beaches, malls, anywhere there were people. So many people are hurting and looking for love in all the wrong places. One day while I was walking down the street, I saw a young pregnant girl. My heart went out to her because she looked to be fifteen and scared. It reminded me of when I was young and pregnant. During my lunch break, I went to sit by the waterside. My thoughts were surrounding the young girl I had seen earlier that day. I began to pray for her. Suddenly, I became consumed with the desire to help young unwed mothers and pregnant girls. I asked God how I could help them; after all, I was once one of them. Then it was as if the light bulb came on inside my head. *Just tell them your story.* I had made many, many mistakes in my life, but God brought me through them all. Now I have a wonderful husband, beautiful twin girls, a son in college with honors, and a successful career, and we have a prominent, growing church.

Soon after that, I became a spokeswoman for the pregnant and young unwed mothers, inspiring them to come up and out of their situations, letting them know that God has a plan for their lives and that pregnancy is not the end for them. I volunteered at the shelters for unwed mothers and shared my story with the girls and young ladies there.

I didn't do this because I felt I had to. I did this because when it was me, I wished someone would have cared enough to do it for me. I even shared with Patience and Grace's friends whenever they had sleepovers, with their parents' permission, of course. Soon it seemed like I was the one people were coming to for advice on raising their teen girls and talking to them about sex, abstinence, and STDs (sexually transmitted diseases). I got brochures from my doctor's office and even got my ob-gyn to come to a meeting we held at church for the young ladies and the young men. I began getting speaking engagements to speak at youth meetings and rallies. I even began working part-time because this got so big. Brandon was now full-time in ministry, so he accompanied me several times on these speaking engagements. I felt like I was contributing to the lives of these young people in a way that they really appreciated. I know I appreciated Brenda and her husband being there for me. One of the things that surprised me was how low these girls' self-esteem was. Many of them had no confidence in themselves. Many felt like the more they gave in to sex, the more they were loved. I was so surprised to find out how many young people thought sex and love were the same thing. Once I thought about it, I realized that we did too when we were teens.

As the years went by, Leroy Jr. graduated from college with honors and was now living on the island of Bermuda, working as an accountant for three law firms. He married a lovely Bermudian girl, Cheryl, who was a wonderful addition to our family.

One day, I had a strange feeling, one I didn't like. My thoughts were on Patience when I woke up. I kept looking at her that morning before she left for school. Somehow, she was different. After the girls left for school, I went into my office to try to do some work on the computer. I couldn't concentrate, so I began to pray. *Lord, what's going on with Patience? Why do I feel this way? I can't shake this feeling that something is wrong, but she looks normal. Lord, if something were wrong, she'd come tell me, wouldn't she? Father, work it all out in Jesus name.*

I just couldn't shake that feeling as the days went by, but

Patience assured me that she was all right. Two and a half months later, while I was at work, Patience called me. She sounded like she had been crying.

I asked, "What's wrong, Patience?"

She asked me if I could come home because she needed to talk to me. She began to cry again.

Now I insisted, "Patience, what's going on? Are you all right?"

She replied, "No!" I paused, and there was complete silence on the phone.

Then I asked the inevitable, "Are you pregnant?" I didn't know why I asked that; she was not even having sex.

To my surprise, she responded, "Yes."

I dropped the phone and then picked it back up. "I'm on my way!" I told her.

Once I had arrived home, I found Patience in her room, curled up on the floor with her pillow.

"Patience," I said. She looked up and saw me and jumped up and ran into my arms. I held her tight. My focus was solely on her. I never even thought about myself or how I felt. "Have you told your father?" I asked.

"No, Mama, just you."

At that moment, Brandon came home and came inside to where we were. "What's going on?" he asked.

So Patience told her father. Brandon and I looked at each other. As Brandon began to hug Patience, he said, "Honey, we will get through this together as a family. We love you, and nothing will ever change that. This too shall pass." Patience cried on her father's chest. "Who is the father, Patience?" Brandon asked.

"Brother and Sister Holmes's son, Malykai," Patience replied.

"Okay, we have to deal with this, Sherri," Brandon said.

When Grace came home, Patience told her. Grace was very supportive of her sister.

That night, Brandon and I had a long talk. During that talk,

I began to think about what people might say. I began to feel embarrassed and ashamed. Here I was, going around preaching and teaching about abstinence, birth control, STDs, and pregnancy, and now my daughter was pregnant. I told Brandon how I was feeling, and he understood and said those thoughts came to him too. He told me that we can only teach them; we can't live their lives for them. They must make their own decisions. That did bring some comfort, but not totally. After we talked, we told the girls that we were going to call Brother and Sister Holmes and meet with them and Malykai. So Brandon called them, and we agreed to meet half an hour later.

They came to our house. Malykai had not told his parents yet, so he took that opportunity to tell them before they came. They were shocked. We all knew Malykai and Patience liked each other but didn't dream they were having sex. Malykai had just turned twenty-one, and Patience and Grace had turned eighteen earlier in the year. The girls were about to graduate from high school, and Malykai was about to graduate from college. Malykai said that he and Patience talked and that he loved her and wanted to marry her. Brandon asked him what kind of plans he had for them.

Malykai said, "I only have three more months of college, and then I will start my career in broadcasting. I am now working part-time at channel 11, and I make twelve dollars an hour. I've saved up a lot of money, and channel 11 wants to keep me on after I graduate. I will work full-time for them, and my salary will increase to thirty-five thousand a year to start. I will get full benefits. Plus I already have insurance, so the baby will be covered."

Brandon was listening intently and then replied, "Let us talk this over with your parents, Malykai. Then we will get back to you and Patience."

Brother Holmes agreed, and then we prayed, and they went home.

It was hard as people found out. I stayed in the word for comfort and strength. I didn't know what people were saying. Patience came to Brandon and me and said she was sorry for getting pregnant and bringing embarrassment and shame to our family and church. It was at that moment that I realized how self-centered I had secretly been. I asked Patience and Brandon to forgive me and then asked God's forgiveness too. What happened, happened. We decided to deal with things the best way we knew how, with lots of love, hugs, and support of one another.

Brother and Sister Holmes invited Brandon and me out for dinner one evening, and we talked about the whole situation. We all admired Malykai for stepping up to do the right thing. As the parents, we decided to present this to Malykai and Patience. We felt that they should both go on and graduate from school and college, and Malykai should continue working and go ahead with his plan for his career. Patience wasn't sure whether she wanted to go to college or not. She said she might go to a trade school. We decided to support them by letting them get married after intense marriage counseling, and they could live with us since we had the space. They could save their money for one year after the baby was born. By then, they should be ready to buy their own home. Both parents would support them and the baby so they could save.

At this time, we began to notice Grace was rebelling a bit. We wondered if she felt we were putting more emphasis on Patience and the baby. Whenever we talked to her about it, she said she was fine, but actions speak louder than words. Grace began hanging out with her friends more and more. We didn't see her much anymore.

The girls graduated, and we gave them a graduation dinner, and we all had lots of fun. Grace introduced a young man to us by the name of Gerald McWilliams. We didn't know him and were concerned because he was so worldly-minded. Grace began acting more and more rebellious. We began hearing her say a lot, "I'm eighteen now."

Leroy Jr. called one night and talked to the girls. When Brandon and I got home, we called him back. He asked us if the girls could come to Bermuda and spend some time there with him and Cheryl. He felt it would be a good change of environment for them and an opportunity to learn about another country and people. We agreed. Patience got an okay from her doctor, and the girls went to Bermuda for a month.

Two days before they were due to leave, Grace told us she was pregnant. Double whammy! That one almost knocked me off my feet. She had decided to have an abortion. When she told us about wanting to have an abortion, I thought to myself, *I don't care.* I was confused myself. I asked God why he was punishing us. Brandon told me I was wrong, and we had a big argument about it. This was our first argument in such a long time. This made Grace feel worse. The next day, I stayed in bed all morning. I couldn't wait for the girls to leave. I lay there in bed thinking about how we had just overcome Patience's pregnancy and now here was Grace with hers. I never in a million years would have thought we would one day be going through this. We had always planned on the girls going to college and meeting their husbands in the church, marrying, *and then* having babies. Suddenly, my thoughts were interrupted by a knock on my bedroom door.

"Who is it?" I asked.

"Grace, can I come in, Mama?"

"Sure," I said coldly.

She came in and hopped right in bed with me and curled up under my covers.

She snuggled up next to me. I smiled as I smelled the fragrance of her hair and thought of when she and Patience did this for years when they were little.

I put my arms around her and said, "What's on my Gracie's mind?"

Then she began to cry. I held her tightly as her body began to shake from the emotion of it all. She said, "Mama, I'm sorry I disappointed you and Daddy. I know I've been acting up lately. I guess I did feel kinda rejected because everyone was talking about Patience, Malykai, and the baby. Mama, please believe me, I didn't do this on purpose. The last thing I want or need is a baby. I don't have someone like Patience who wants to marry me. I just wish I could do it all over again, Mama. I'd do it different."

My heart began to melt as I held my baby in my arms again and heard myself nineteen years earlier when I was pregnant. I remembered I thought about abortion and quickly dismissed it because I had grown to realize that an unborn baby is a baby full of life. The key word was *life*. And because of that decision, I now had Patience and Grace. What if I had aborted them? Oh, I hated to think of that. Suddenly, I realized it's not about what people think. This child inside of Grace had no one to speak up for him or her, someone to say, "Hey, I'm here and full of life. I love you, Mommy, save me and don't abort me." Some of my own words came back to me, and I realized the focus should be on the baby too. Sure, abstinence is the best way, but I had to realize that some people were going to have sex anyway and get pregnant or get someone pregnant. Once that happens, what about the baby? Someone needed to speak for the unborn too. Wow, this was really deep to me. Suddenly, Brandon came in and sat on the side of the bed and said to Grace, "That is our grandchild inside of you, and we love him or her. Grace, you are going to be a mother, and your child needs you to love and care for him while he is inside of you. Sweetheart, you don't know who you are carrying, what gifts they possess, or how many lives they will influence for good. Do your part and nurture your child and give him the best you can. Give him Jesus."

Grace was really crying by now.

Patience came to the door and said, "What's going on in here?" When she saw her sister crying, she wanted to know what was wrong. She came over to hug her sister. "We're here for you, Gracie, and always will be," Patience said.

I slid from under the covers, and Brandon and I walked out and left the girls in there, consoling each other.

"Honey," I said, "I'm sorry for arguing with you. You were right, and I was wrong. Please forgive me."

Brandon replied, "Of course, I forgive you, baby. I hate to argue with you. Honey, it's important for the girls to always know that we love and support them and one another. Understand, baby, we're not supporting what they did, we're supporting them through their pregnancies to do the right thing. We are family, and these babies will be born into a loving family."

When the girls left for Bermuda, it was a bittersweet moment. Now Brandon and I could have some much-needed time to ourselves to sort through things and prepare for what was next. At the same time, I knew this was a crucial time for Grace. She was at a point where she was fragile, and I knew it could go either way, good or bad. I had to trust God!

Leroy Jr. and Cheryl met the girls at the airport, and they were all excited. They hadn't seen each other in over a year. The girls fell in love with Bermuda, its crystal clear blue water, the beaches, the white roofs on the brightly colored houses, the people, and their foods. They thought it was all so beautiful. When they called us to let us know they arrived safely, Brandon and I decided we're going to take our vacation there in the fall.

As time went by, God helped me; and to my surprise, our church family was very supportive, and so were my coworkers. Of course, there were those who were negative, but like Brandon said, we are family, and we are here for one another. Even Leroy was supportive through it all. God taught me valuable lessons about self-centeredness, pride, and false humility. I had to repent. When the girls saw me again, they saw a new mother. When we saw the girls again, we saw new daughters. We got a surprise we were not expecting.

While the girls were in Bermuda, they met Cheryl's grandmother, Mother Pearl Walker. She was a seasoned little woman of God who loved the youth. She and the girls developed a bond, and they adopted her as their grandmother. Mother Walker shared with the girls about her own life and how Jesus was the one to help her through. She shared with the girls about the love of God and all she has seen God do for herself and others. She took the girls to revival with her and introduced them to the youth of her church. There the girls met people and made lasting friendships. We were told Grace cried for the first three nights of revival, and then on the fourth night, Mother Walker led her to the Lord. Patience followed on the fifth night. Mother Walker has made a huge impact on the girls' lives. Brandon and I are so grateful that no matter where your children are, God is there too.

So this brings us up to today. Patience had a baby girl, Amber Dawn Holmes. Two months later, Grace had a baby boy, Jonathan Blake Williamson. We invited Mother Walker to come with Leroy Jr. and Cheryl when the girls had the babies and for Patience and Malykai's wedding. So we were able to meet the woman who led our girls to Christ. Mother Walker has become a very special part of our family. Leroy and Brandon both gave Patience away, one on each arm. Everyone is doing great. Malykai and Patience have had challenges, but their love is so strong they'll make it through anything. Grace had Jonathan and went on to college. She is still there and doing well. She is studying to become a registered nurse. Yesterday, Grace told us she met a single, saved doctor at the hospital who was from Bermuda. He wanted to take her out and meet her son. "God, let your will be done!" Leroy Jr. and Cheryl have a son of their own now, and his name is Leroy III. Brandon and I have bought a cottage in Bermuda and go there twice a year for some R & R (rest and relaxation). The double whammy has turned into a double blessing, Amber and Jonathan.

Selah

Mother Alma Rogers*

In the Amplified Bible, Psalm 90:10a says, "The days of our years are threescore years and ten (seventy years)." In Matthew 18:21–22, we read, "Then Peter came to him and said, 'Lord, how many times may my brother sin against me and I forgive him and let it go? [as many as] up to seven times?' "Jesus answered him, 'I tell you, not up to seven times, but seventy times seven!"

In Luke 17:3 and 4 (NKJV), Jesus said, "Take heed to yourselves, If your brother sins against you, rebuke him; and if he repents, forgive him. And if he sins against you seven times in a day, and seven times in a day returns to you saying, 'I repent,' you shall forgive him."

We will look at several points from these scriptures. For now, let us take a look at them from a mathematical perspective.

1 year = 365 days (not including leap year)
70 years = 25,550 days
70 x 7 times to forgive = 490 times in 1 day
490 x 25,550 = 12,519,500

Does that sound like a lot of forgiving for just one person? *Remember this:*

If Jesus said it, you can do it.

~Selah~ (think calmly about it)

What does it mean to forgive? We examined how many times we should forgive each other. We discovered that we are expected to forgive one person up to 490 times a day and over 12,000,000 times in a lifetime if necessary. Now let's look at what it means to forgive.

To forgive means to cease feeling resentment against an offender, to not seek revenge, to not expect to make someone else pay for what they did against you. In other words, it means to remove someone from blame or responsibility of the outcome of an offense.

In Luke 17:1–4 (NKJV), Jesus told his disciples,

"It is impossible that no offenses should come, but woe to him through whom they do come. It would be better for him if a millstone were hung around his neck and he were thrown into the sea, than that he should offend one of these little ones. Take heed to yourselves. If your brother sins against you rebuke him; and if he repents, forgive him."

Let's look at a few facts:

1. Jesus was talking to *his* disciples, the ones who subscribed to his teachings and called him master. If this happened today, we could say that Jesus would be talking to born again believers who have accepted him as "Savior" and "Lord."
2. We can expect offenses to come. Sometimes people know when they offend us, but sometimes they don't.
3. When people offend us, we should rebuke them or reprove them for it. Don't act as though nothing has happened when you feel hurt or offended.

4. If he repents or shows regret for offending or hurting you, Jesus has commanded you to forgive him. Notice he didn't say, "You may if you want to" or "You should forgive." He said, "If he repents, *forgive* him."

Perhaps you are wondering what you should do if the offender knows that he has offended you but does not repent. I believe we are still to rebuke and forgive. It is not our job to retaliate or return evil for evil. According to verse 2 of our scripture, their punishment is preplanned, and it is worse than what we could do to them.

Remember this: As a disciple of Jesus Christ, we are commanded to forgive and not to pay back.

~Selah~

Questions to Consider

Is there someone in your life that you need to forgive?

Do you find it extremely difficult to let go of the past?

Has there been a situation in your life that has left you struggling with forgiving yourself?

Are you blaming God for something that happened in your life?

Once you make the decision and forgive, ask God, "What am I to learn from this whole situation?"

Forgive and be free!

*Now deceased

Careful, You Might Get What You Say

"Ask and it will be given to you; seek and you will
find; knock and the door will be opened to you."
Matthew 7:7 NIV

I could never understand why my single Christian friends had such a hard time remaining celibate while waiting to be married. It seemed to me that they had so much time to spend with the Lord in prayer and service for the Lord. I wished I had that kind of time. What was the big deal? Single people had it so easy; on the other hand, I had a husband, children, job, and church responsibilities to cater to. My marriage was in serious trouble, which took a lot of my time and made me weary mentally.

Greg, my husband, had a roaming eye, and I had just learned he had roaming hands too. My friend at church, Rachel, told me to watch Greg the next time we had visitors at church and he hugged the females. Of course, that made me angry and defensive of my husband, but I must admit, I was curious. Rachel knew Greg and I were having problems and told me she never liked him anyway but accepted him because he was my husband. She said she didn't trust him. Obviously, she was jealous of us. I didn't really understand why, maybe because I had a husband and she didn't; there was no other explanation. She told me to brace myself for what I was going to see.

On Sunday, Pastor Sims from Pilgrim Baptist Church was going to be preaching in the afternoon and bringing his congregation. That week prior was a very busy week preparing for the special service and visitors, but we had fun, though, cleaning, decorating, and practicing the choir, all in preparation for the afternoon service. Meanwhile, at home, Greg and I seemed to be on a good path. We were getting along better, and it actually seemed like we were having a turnaround in our marriage.

Sunday afternoon as we, the choir, were singing and having a good time, some of Pastor Sims's members came in and were escorted to the front of the church and were seated in the section prepared for them. Among them were three nicely dressed ladies. One, in particular, was a young woman dressed like she had just left the club or was going there right after church. Her dress was so tight you couldn't help but see every curve her curvaceous body displayed. You could tell she felt uncomfortable because she kept pulling on the length of her dress as if that would hide the shortness of it resting on her mid-thigh. There is something about being in the presence of the Lord that makes you feel exposed.

When the service was over, I looked for Greg so we could leave, and from a distance, I saw him approaching the three ladies; he seemed so nice and friendly. I saw my husband, but he was acting like someone I had never seen before. He was smiling as he approached them. I didn't know what was being said, but I knew what I saw. What I saw hurt to the core of my soul. Greg, I suppose, was introducing himself to them as one of the leaders as he always did. One of the women extended her hand to him to shake it, and he reached out and grabbed her and embraced her. Okay, no big deal; we embrace in our church. Greg turned to the woman with the club outfit on, and I saw him smile and say something to her that made her blush, and then he reached out to embrace her. Then I saw it. He had both his hands on the top of her back and then slid them down slowly and rested them on the top of her bubble butt and kept them there for a few seconds. He was looking right in her face as he held his hands there and said something to her before releasing them. It felt like a ton of bricks had just fallen on me. I couldn't believe what I had just seen. I watched for a few more moments, and the women turned to leave. At that point, I felt it. It came so silently, so subtly, without warning. It was *betrayal*. First of all, he had no right to do that to her. What was even more painful was that was the way he held me when he was being romantic. I picked up the kids from children's church and went to the car and sat there a moment, thinking, before driving home without him.

When I got home, I got the children ready and in bed because I knew it was going to be a big fight when Greg got home. I took a shower to try to cool off and calm down. With the water running down my face, I cried so hard until I felt weak. I got out of the shower, feeling defeated at the thought of my husband's hands on another woman's butt. I thought we were doing better, but now I was beginning to feel bitter. Just then, Rachel called, asking me what happened to me. She had brought the purse I had asked to borrow but couldn't find me after service. Without answering her, I said, "Rachel, what happened with Greg to make you tell me what you said about visiting women?" Rachel was silent for a moment and slowly said, "Trish, what happened? Did you see or hear something?" I begged her to just tell me what happened. She said she didn't want to put our friendship at risk again. I assured her it wouldn't be.

She told me a woman from Pentecost Cathedral saw her at the mall and introduced herself by reminding her she was with the group that sang at our church last month. She asked about Greg by asking Rachel if she had his phone number. Rachel told me that Greg asked for her phone number, but she refused to give it to him and instead asked for his and said she'd call him. She said her phone got wet, and she lost all the numbers in it. Rachel told her that was God because Greg was married to her best friend. The woman was so ashamed and said that she had no idea he was married and that she would never be the cause of destroying a family because she wouldn't want that done to her. The woman told Rachel she felt sorry for me because Greg acts nothing like a married man. She told her when he hugged her after service, he slid his hands down her back and rested them on the top of her butt and told her that she was one of the most beautiful women he had seen in a long time and that she had the most beautiful eyes he had ever seen. He said he wanted to get to know her better and asked for her number.

Rachel admitted she was angry and tried to tell me right away. She said she had second thoughts because of the way I reacted when she told me the little she had, so she just told me to watch how he treats visiting women. She decided not to risk our fourteen-year friendship by telling me everything she knew. At first, I was mad at her for not telling me, but after a moment of consideration, I knew she made the right decision. Now I realized she saw something in Greg I was blind to. I was so protective of my husband and children, and she knew that. Just then, I heard Greg coming in and told her to pray because I knew we were about to have probably the biggest fight we had ever had.

Greg came to our room, fuming with anger. "Why did you leave me, woman?" I told him to lower his tone and not to wake the children. This man was incredible, and I don't mean in a good way. He actually denied doing what I saw him do and stated I was only seeing what I wanted to see. I told him that was the last thing I wanted to see especially since we seemed to be turning things around in our marriage. The argument got really heated and intense and ended with Greg sleeping in our guest room. Long story short, in the end, Greg and I divorced, and I got custody of the children and the house. We both decided it would be in the best interest of the children not to uproot them and have them start in another school on top of their parents divorcing.

I must admit it was hard . . . really hard, but as time went by, it eventually got better. I had to focus on my children and try to make things good while they adjusted. Eventually, they were doing better and saw their father on weekends, and before I realized it, two years had gone by. Rachel stayed in my corner all the way through. She gave me a book entitled *Forgiving Is Easy . . . Or Is It*," and after reading it, I decided to forgive Greg and asked God to help me to do that. I'm not sure when it happened, but I just knew that I didn't feel anger anymore toward him. I didn't feel anything. I just hoped he would come to grips with himself and ask God to help him. Hallelujah, I felt free in my heart to move on.

R & R

One day, Rachel called and asked if I wanted to go to Florida with her for ten days for some rest and relaxation; R & R she called it. I checked my schedule and worked it out with Greg and my mother to keep the children while I was gone. I couldn't think of the last time I had done something like this. The closer it got to the time to leave, the more excited I became. All I could think about was spending quiet time in the hotel room, swimming, and shopping. I just wanted to laugh and have some chill time with my bestie!

The night before we left, Greg came to pick up the children. While I was gathering their things, he asked me why we were going to Florida for some R & R. I turned to look at him in shock. He asked why we wouldn't just go to a hotel here. I told him it was our choice, and frankly, it was none of his business. He said he was just concerned about our safety and all since we were two women traveling alone. Then he said something that totally blew me away. He asked if I had been working out because I looked really good. I just stood there looking at him in disbelief and asked him where all this was coming from. He came over to me, standing in my personal space, and put one hand on my shoulder and said in an all too familiar voice, low and sweet, "I'm so glad you are the mother of my children. I can't think of anyone else I would want to have had children with." He then put his other hand on my other shoulder and gently pulled me close to him while staring in my eyes. I was mesmerized because I heard the Greg I had married. He gently put his arms around me, touching the top of my back, and ran them down my back, resting them on my hips at my waistline. He then stepped in and pressed his body against mine. He said, "I was a fool to let you go. Trish, you're so beautiful." Then he slid his hands around, resting them on the top of my butt. He leaned into my ear and said, "I've been thinking about you so much and remembering how you feel and taste. I'm so sorry for all the wrong I've done to you and the hurt I've caused you. You didn't deserve any of it, and I was a total jerk. Trish, please forgive me."

I was frozen for a moment as many thoughts flooded my mind. Then I remembered those were the very moves that led to the biggest fight we had ever had and ultimately our divorce. I pulled away from him and looked at him in anger and said, "Don't ever put your hands on me again. I'm not your wife anymore. I forgave you a long time ago, but that doesn't mean I have to let you back into my heart. In fact, I'm doing just fine without you." I told him to take the children and leave. He looked at me, and this time, he looked hurt. He said to me, "You're different." I told him I did a lot of growing up since we were divorced and didn't want to go through any of that again. Greg insisted that he had changed, and I told him I was glad he changed. Maybe now he would be a better husband to someone else. He wanted to know why we couldn't be friends. I told him that though I forgave him, the pain was so deep that I didn't want to take the chance of him hurting me again, and besides that, I didn't trust him. He said okay and that he could see I needed more time to think about it. I shook my head and just walked away. As he and the children were walking to the car, he turned around and said to me, "Don't do anything I wouldn't do." I said in return, "That's a loaded statement, and I make no promises." I only said that to get to him.

Florida, Here We Come!

Rachel and I were so excited about our trip. This was something we both needed because of our busy schedules. I hadn't been on a solo trip without the children in such a long time. In fact, I couldn't even remember a time I did since they were born. Once we were on the plane, seated and in the air, Rachael asked me, "What happened last night when Greg came over to pick up the children?" I asked her to promise me that she wouldn't mention him again during this entire trip. I told her, "My name ain't Stella, but I'm trying to get my groove back." Rachael responded, "Oooooh, girl, I'm scared of you! Watch out, Florida, here comes Trish!" We both laughed and clicked our paper airplane cups containing Sprite. I told her I wanted to get the makeover I saw in the brochure included with the information concerning our all-inclusive package. We had been meeting up at the gym pretty consistently during our lunch hour for the past five months, and it had really paid off.

The resort we were staying at was simply beautiful! I planned to take full advantage of this all-inclusive package. The sun was shining, and the sky was blue with a few snow-white clouds. The little breeze blowing was warm, but we didn't care; we brought bathing suits! We got checked in and changed into them and went directly to the pool, which was closed in by glass. The view from the pool was the ocean, and it was spectacular. I felt relaxed already just taking in the scene. As we reclined in the lounge chairs, I closed my eyes, took a deep breath, and let it out slowly. A young man came to us, carrying a pad of paper and a pen. He said, "Excuse me, ladies." I opened my eyes and saw a beautiful man dressed in a tight white T-shirt and khaki shorts. He said, "My name is Fritz. Would you ladies like something to drink?" Rachel saw him, sat up, and said, "Mmmm, are you the cabana boy?" Fritz smiled and said, "Not at all. I'm just here to help make your trip a bit more pleasurable." Rachel then said as she looked intently at this man, "So you are the cabana boy!" I spoke up and said, "Don't mind her. She doesn't get out often." Rachel said, "True, and neither do you, Stella!" Fritz laughed and said, "Oooh, I see, you ladies are here to get your groove back." I felt so embarrassed, but clearly, Rachel didn't. She laughed with him and said, "I'll take an iced tea, but please pass by Long Island and don't stop! We're good Christian girls." Fritz looked a bit puzzled and said, "Oh okay." Then he turned to me and asked me if I wanted anything. I said, "I'll take a Sprite please." When he left us, I told Rachel she was crazy. I said, "He must think we're desperate, and that is so not the case." Rachel laughed and said, "Speak for yourself. I'm gonna be good, but I'm not going to act all stuffy and stuck up. I came to have fun, and fun I will have. And so will you, Trish."

    I got up and went into the pool and swam. When I got out, Fritz was with Rachel, serving our drinks. I asked him if he knew of any nice shops or boutiques. Then I apologized. He asked why I was apologizing. I told him, "You are a man and probably wouldn't know about those things. I'll ask the lady at the front desk." Fritz said, "No, you don't want to ask her. She won't send you to where I'll send you. My sister happens to own a boutique about a mile south of here. It's across the street from the beach too. It's called Lola's Boutique. If you ladies decide to go, tell her Fritz sent you. Rachel said, "That sounds great!! We'll look her up and go tomorrow. I just want to finish up this day right here at this pool, get something to eat, and come right back here and watch the sun go down." Fritz wrote down the phone number to his sister's boutique and gave it to us. He also told us the sunset was so beautiful from here. He further told us they open the glass wall facing the ocean so the ocean breeze can be felt. "There's always a breeze off the ocean that can be felt right here. I think you ladies will enjoy it! We have a live jazz band that plays smooth jazz, and some folks even step out onto the beach and dance." We thanked Fritz, and he began to walk away and then turned around and said, "Hey, I don't even know your names." Rachel said, "I'm Rachel, and this is Stella!" Fritz and Rachel laughed, and I just shook my head in disbelief that she said that. I extended my hand to him, shook his, and said, "My name is Trish. Just Trish." Then we all laughed as Fritz walked away.

Rachel and I decided to have dinner at the restaurant there. We had lobster and champagne. I told her I was two years late, but I was celebrating freedom and new beginnings. She laughed at me and said, "Really, girl, after two years? You've *been* free. Thank God!" "Yea," I said, "but I've never felt as free as I do now. I don't know. Maybe it's because the children aren't with me." "Probably so," Rachel said, "because you always have them, and on weekends when you don't, you're still working." I laughed and said, "Look who's talking, Ms. Overachiever herself!" She raised her glass and said, "And that's why we can do what we're doing!" This time, we clicked champagne goblets as we laughed and planned out our day tomorrow.

We went back to the pool, and the vibe was really nice. Jazz music, an absolute brilliant red and orangey gold sky as the sun was setting, along with gentle ocean breezes. Fritz was right; this was beautiful. Well, actually, it was better than that! As we reclined, once again, I closed my eyes and felt total serenity. I took a deep breath and released it slowly. Then I heard, "Would you ladies like to dance?" I opened my eyes again, and there were two good-looking men standing there. "Sure," Rachel said. As we stood up, the men introduced themselves to us as London Cooper and David August. Rachel and David danced, and London and I danced. We ended up sitting by the pool with David and London until 2:00 a.m. I must admit, we had so much fun with them. They seemed really down to earth. London told me they were from California and had just that day ended the business portion of their trip and now had three free personal days before they headed back to Cali. He said they worked in real estate and were there for a convention along with others and to close on some property their company bought for retail purposes. They apparently wanted to open another location in Florida. They asked us if we wanted to have lunch with them later, and Rachel suggested an early dinner so we could go sleep in and then go shopping. We all agreed, and the guys walked us to our room and said good night.

After we had brunch, we decided to take the resort van down to Lola's Boutique and shop. The boutique was located in a shopping/touristy area, so we knew we'd be there a while. On our way out, we saw Fritz. He smiled and waved to us as we approached him. "Well, hello, Trish and Rachel. Did you ladies enjoy the sunset last night?" "Oh yes, we did," I said. "Thanks for telling us about the night activities here." Fritz replied, "I remembered Rachel saying you are Christians, so I didn't suggest the clubs here because they can get pretty wild. Are you going to see my sister today?" "Yes," Rachel responded, "in fact, that's where we're headed now." Fritz told us he'd give his sister a heads-up about our coming and to treat us well. "Enjoy your day, ladies. Have fun!" Fritz said. As we walked toward the van, I turned around to look at Fritz in his uniform, a tight white T-shirt and khaki shorts. *That sure is a good-looking man*, I thought. Rachel said, "Okay, I see you, girl! And yes, he is fine!" "Is it that obvious?" I said. Rachel said it was to her because she knew me very well.

This whole trip was turning out to be so much fun. We reached Lola's Boutique, and when we entered, we were greeted by Lola herself. "Hi," she said. "You must be the ladies from the resort my brother works at. Welcome to Lola's Boutique! Feel free to look around, and if you see something you like but don't see your size, let me know. We have inventory in the back." Now we were in our element! We loved to shop, and we especially loved boutique shopping because at times you could find one-of-a-kind pieces, and Lola's Boutique was filled with them. We even got some shoes as well. Lola was really cool too. She was about our age and asked how we were enjoying our trip so far. We told her we were having a great time and now, thanks to her brother, found a great place to shop and a great new friend. "My brother told me you are Christians. My church is having a special service on Saturday night, and I'd like to invite you guys to come. Here's the information. If you care to fit it in your schedule, feel free to stop by. You won't regret it." We told her we'd see how things go. She gave us the names of a few more shops she thought we'd like now that she had an idea of our taste. She offered us a beverage before we headed out and told us to tell Fritz she said hello. We shopped and bought souvenirs. I also picked up some things for the children. I didn't remember the last time I felt so free; this was great!

We got back to the resort, and there was Fritz. For some reason, I found him so interesting. I didn't know why because he didn't really do anything other than be nice, and I guessed that was part of his job. Nonetheless, he caught my attention. "Good afternoon, Trish, Rachel. Did you ladies have a good time? I'm going to guess you had a great time, judging by the bags you're carrying." He said this as he motioned for a young man to bring the cart over for us to put our things on. "We had a great time, and your sister is so nice. She invited us to her church on Saturday," Rachel said. Then I asked, "Do you go to that church, Fritz?" I wasn't sure why I held my breath waiting for his answer. When he said yes, I let the air out as a sigh of relief. Just then, I noticed the huge clock on the wall and told Rachel we'd better hurry so we wouldn't be late meeting London and David. Fritz escorted us to our room, pushing the cart with our belongings on it. He said, "Oh, you met the group here for the real estate convention?" Rachel said, "No, we only met two of them, David August and London Cooper. Have you met them, Fritz?" Fritz said he met the whole group but not the two men personally. When we got to our room, he told us to have fun and stay safe. He looked at me and said, "Remember you're Trish and not Stella." Then he winked his eye and smiled. It was then that I noticed he had dimples. In fact, in that brief moment, I noticed a lot about Fritz. He had a beautiful, smooth tan skin, white teeth, and a well-groomed close-cut full beard, and his brown hair had streaks of blond highlights. He had an athletic frame and nice calf muscles. *Okay, okay, girl*, I thought. I had to interrupt my thoughts. I had never been into a white man before, but suddenly, I was drawn to him.

Rachel and I changed and met London and David in the lounge. We decided to take a walk on the beach before going to the Lobster House on the beachfront. While London and I were walking and talking, he told me he thought I was a very attractive and sophisticated woman. He said he could tell that I was smart and savvy. At that moment, the ocean breeze blew my hat off. London went chasing it and brought it back to me. "Thank you, sir," I said as I smiled at him. He asked me if I worked out, and I told him yes. He said, "I can tell because you are toned and look good in everything I've seen you wear. You're a beautiful woman, Trish. I can't believe you have three children. And this outfit you're wearing now isn't making you. Girl, you're making it." London sure knew how to make a lady feel good, and I told him so. He said, "I'm only telling the truth. If I didn't believe it, I wouldn't say anything about it. But to be quite frank, Trish, you are fine!" I couldn't help blushing. Then he leaned in and gently kissed my cheek. That made me feel good, but I hadn't let anyone get too much further past this point since my divorce. My guard was always up to protect not only myself but also my children. But this time, this trip, I was going to trust and let my guard down. London was really sweet and easy to talk to. He reached out and put his arm around my waist, and I stopped him. "Hey, what are you doing?" I asked. He said, "Trish, I'm not going to lie. I like you. You are a beautiful woman and a great person. I can tell you're a good mother. I don't know why you're not married, but that's good for me." I asked him why. He continued, "I'd like to get to know you better. I hope you don't think I'm moving too fast, but I don't want to leave Florida and never see or talk to you again. He then tried again and put his arm around my waist, and I let him.

Dinner was fun! We danced, and we let the guys talk us into having a drink or two. I was never a drinker, so London suggested a fruity drink. It was okay. I just drank it. He said, "Hey, slow down there, lady. Sip your drink. Now I have to get you another one 'cause you just drank that one down. LOL!" Rachel clearly was into David and vice versa. After dinner, we went to a comedy club and laughed 'til our stomachs hurt. Then we went back to the resort, and London and I decided to sit at the pool and enjoy the band, ocean breezes, and each other's company. David and Rachel went somewhere else. Then London walked me to my room. We had such a wonderful night. I was feeling so good, and London kept telling me how beautiful and sexy I was. When we got to my room, London kissed me, and we were both feeling it, so he made his way into my room where we had a very passionate night. He left around 4:00 a.m. when Rachel came in. Once he was gone, Rachel and I sat there, looking at each other, and slowly, I asked, "Did you?" She glared at me and shook her head up and down. "Me too," I replied. She looked shocked, and we were silent until we fell asleep.

At noon, there was a knock on our door. It was David. He wanted to see Rachel. I told him she was still asleep and I'd have her call him when she was awake. He said okay and left. When I went back, I saw Rachel sitting up in her bed. I said, "Sorry, did I wake you?" She said the knock on the door woke her and she didn't feel like going back to sleep. My head was hurting, so I called down to the front to ask for some headache medicine. They said they would bring some right away. "Rach, I can't believe I did that. It's been so long." "Yeah, same here, but I don't know about the so long part." I looked at her and said, "What does that mean?" She said, "I don't tell you *everything*." "So you're not celibate?" I asked. Rachel drew her knees up to her chest and wrapped her arms around them and rested her chin on top of her knees and said, "Nope." I was shocked. "Girl, I'm your best friend. How come I didn't know that?" I woke completely up at this point. She said she knew I was doing the celibate thing and didn't want to discourage me. "I'm not like you, Trish. I wish I could be celibate, but I like having a man in my bed. There I said it. Don't judge me." I just sat there with my mouth open. "Trish, can I ask you something?" "Sure," I said. "What was it like for you after all this time?" Just then, a member of the hotel staff came to the door with the medicine for my headache. I had almost forgotten about my headache after hearing what Rachel had to say. I took the medicine along with half a blueberry bagel and some water. I went back over to where Rachel was, and she said, "Well, are you going to answer my question?" I sat in the chair over by the window and looked out at the ocean and said, "It was actually wonderful, but I feel so guilty. He was better than I've ever had. Rach, you know what's so scary about this is that I could get used to it. So I won't see London again." Rachel looked at me in disbelief. "Girl, are you crazy? You like him. He likes you. What's the problem?" "I'm saved!" I said loudly. She retorted back, "I am too!" We both were silent for a moment.

Then I said, "Okay, I won't judge you and please don't judge me either." "Deal," she said.

I went and took a shower. While there, I prayed and told God I was sorry for having sex with London. "God, please forgive me. Greg was good, but London was way better." Wow! Maybe it was because it had been so long, but some things you just don't forget. I told God I wouldn't do it again and felt better after having my talk with him. God is so good like that.

I got dressed while Rachel was in the shower. I did my hair and put on a little makeup. I called to check up on the children while Rachel got dressed. They were with my mother, so I called her. I didn't want to call while they were with Greg. He would asked all kinds of questions, and I didn't want to hear them. I asked Rachel if I could borrow some of her jewelry, and she wore some of mine. We were like that with each other, like sisters, but we didn't fight. She called David, and they wanted to go to the beach and hang out with us again. I was a bit hesitant but agreed. We met them in the lobby. We got there first, and I saw Fritz again. Rachel teased me and said, "Girl, here comes your other man." "Ha, ha!" I said. "Hey, Trish, wow, you're a very pretty lady, but you look extra pretty today." "Thank you," I said as I tried to hide my blush. "Rachel, how are you today?" "Great!" she replied. "So what exciting things do you ladies have planned for today? More shopping?" Fritz asked. Just at that moment, London and David walked up to us. Talk about awkward. Fritz spoke to the men and said, "Oh, you guys are going out together?" He looked almost hurt. I couldn't take it, so I moved toward the door. Rachel came with me, and we left the men there, talking. We took the van to the beach, and London kept trying to get close and cozy with me, but I resisted . . . a little. I couldn't help it; this man was so, so, so . . . I don't know. I just couldn't think of the right words. But I did like the way he made me feel. We had so much fun at the beach, and then we went and got a burger and fries at the Burger Shack at the other end of the beach. The guys rented two of those Japanese tricycles with the Japanese rider pedaling, and they took us to the Burger Shack. From there, we went to the Aquarium and then did some more shopping.

We then took a tour bus around the area and saw some of the most beautiful houses. Some were even owned by celebrities. After a full day, we headed back to the resort to change and go to dinner. London kissed me, and I went into my room. Rachel came in a little later as she was down at the pool with David. Then there was a knock on my door; it was London. I opened it, and he came in and gave me a real kiss. Long and passionate. This man right here was something else. What was happening to me? When it came to him, I found myself feeling weak. He turned to leave, and I shocked myself by reaching out and grabbing him and pulling him to me, and that was it. Here we go again. It felt so good being in his arms.

He left to go to his room to shower and change. Rachel came in about five minutes after he left. She was smiling. I looked at her and laughed. She said, "Why are you laughing?" I told her I recognized that look. "What were you and David doing? Hmmmm?" Then we both laughed. While we were getting ready for dinner, we talked about how much fun we were having. David called Rachel and said to come to their room. He said they had ordered dinner and wanted us to come to their room. So we went to join them in their room where there was a very elegant candle lit dinner waiting for us out on their patio overlooking the pool. We could hear the jazz music playing, which helped create the atmosphere. Once again, we had a wonderful time with the guys. They had wine, so I felt it was okay to have some. I figured I wouldn't get a headache from wine. The guys said they were leaving Friday, so we had one more day together. It was obvious David and Rachel were going to keep in touch. London said he wanted to as well. I went to the bathroom and saw a picture of

London, another woman, and two children. I felt a sinking feeling in the pit of my stomach. I wondered who she and the children were. I picked the picture up and couldn't help but notice all the children looked like London. *Oh god*, I thought. *Please don't let this man be married.* When I asked him earlier when we met if he was married, he said no. When I returned to the group, I was distant in my thoughts because I kept wondering about the picture I saw. So I asked London privately again if he was married. He looked puzzled. "Why are you asking me that question again? I already told you I wasn't." So I told him about the picture I saw in the bathroom.

"You went through my stuff?" he shouted. "No, it was just lying there on the shelf. And don't shout at me again. All I did was ask you a question." That was a vibe killer. I lost interest at that point. I couldn't believe he shouted at me. I didn't do anything wrong; he's the one that left it there. "I'm sorry for shouting at you, Trish." I looked at London and told him I wasn't feeling it anymore. "I can't believe you yelled at me. And what reason would I have to go through your things? I'm not that kind of person." London reached out to take my hand, but I pulled away. "Trish, I'm sorry. I really am. Come on, let's go back out on the patio with David and Rachel." I went, but that kept bothering me for some reason. I just couldn't cozy up to London anymore. So I told them I was going back to the room, and he said he'd walk me there. While we walked, he asked me what was wrong. I asked him who the people in the picture were. He said they were his sister and her children. "Why are you taking a picture with your sister and her children? That's unusual, and you brought it on a trip with you?" I said. I got a strange feeling in my gut. I felt like I'd made the biggest mistake of my life, and I told him. "Do you really feel that way?" London asked. "I thought we were having fun. I know I was. Don't mess things up by bringing her into this." "Your sister?" I said. London took a deep breath and said, "No, my wife." I was dumbfounded. Speechless and just numb. He continued, "We're getting a divorce. I met you and was so attracted to you. Please don't be upset with me. Like I said, we're getting a divorce." I was so angry, and just knowing what all we'd done made me angrier. I would never do that to someone knowingly. "Divorce or not, London, how could you do that to me? I can't undo what's already been done, but I cannot see you again. I wish I'd never met you, and I don't ever want to see you again. I went into my room and cried and cried and cried.

Rachel came in to check on me. She said, "London came in upset and said he never meant to hurt you. I asked him what happened, and he told me to ask you." "Rachel, he's married!" I said through my tears. "What?" Rachel shouted. "Trish, I'm so sorry," she said, hugging me. "I better not find out David is too. But wait, he knew London was married and went along with it all. As far as I'm concerned, he's just as guilty. If he'd hide something as precious as that, that tells me his regard for marriage isn't too high. I want to go back there and tell them both a few things." I told her it wouldn't do any good and it's not worth it. "I'm just done with them. I can't believe I let myself do this. Oh, God, I'm so sorry!" I yelled out. The pain was so deep. I fell for the trap the enemy laid out for me and slept with someone else's husband. David tried calling Rachel, but she would not respond to his calls.

I hardly slept that night. I finally fell asleep around 6:00 a.m. I woke up around noon to a knock on the door. I heard Rachel say, "Hi, Fritz." Oh no, I thought, I didn't want to see Fritz. It just felt like everyone who looked at me would know I had slept with a married man... *twice*! Rachel came in and saw I was awake and said Fritz came to remind us of the service at their church tomorrow night. I told Rachel, "I just want to go home. I don't want to see London or David, let alone Fritz." Rachel told me to just go back to sleep or she could order some food for us. I told her I wasn't hungry. I was so ashamed of myself for following a stupid feeling I felt from a guy I didn't even know. "Trish, maybe it would be good for us to go to that service. I, for one, feel like I need to be around other believers right about now. I need to be grounded." I told her I'd see how I felt later. I decided to grab my Bible, which I hadn't looked at since I'd arrived. That was part of the problem, I told myself. I should have been in the word every day. I really had been acting like Stella. "Father," I prayed, "please forgive me for all the wrong I've done. Make things right within my heart and take this pain away. Should we go to the service tomorrow night at Fritz and Lola's church? Let me know, Father, in Jesus's name, Amen."

Suddenly, I just wanted to go shopping back at Lola's Boutique. So we got ready and headed down to the lobby to get the van. There was Fritz, and I surely didn't want to speak to him. But that wouldn't be fair; he did nothing wrong. He approached us cautiously. "Good afternoon, Rachel. Good afternoon, Trish." He looked at me and asked if I was all right. "Hi, Fritz. What makes you think I'm not?" "Look, I can say this to you because I know you'd understand, but you were on my mind all night. I don't mean that disrespectfully. I kept waking up feeling I should pray for you. I just felt like you were in trouble or something. Are you okay?" I looked at him in the eyes, and I saw genuine concern, nothing else. I instantly felt peace and thanked him for his prayers. "Wow," Rachel said in amazement. She stood there with her mouth slightly opened. I said, "I was a bit upset last night and disappointed, but once again, God showed me how much he loves me. Thank you, Fritz, for praying for me." "You're welcome anytime, anytime. I follow his lead when I hear the Father." Fritz gently took my hand and softly said, "Father, be with these ladies today. Protect and please comfort their hearts in Jesus's name. Amen." We thanked Fritz again and got on the van in silence. As we traveled up the road, Rachel broke the silence by saying, "If I weren't there, I don't know if I would have believed it. That was such an intense moment. I mean God is so intense. Wow, what a guy." I said, "You mean what a God! I'm still trying to wrap my head around it, Rach. God is so intentionally intense. Wow!" We rode the rest of the way in silence, thinking of the goodness of God and how it is true. No matter what we do or what we've done, he never leaves us or forsakes us. God just proved that to us personally. Somehow, I could feel my heart mending.

When we arrived at Lola's Boutique, she was waiting with cold glasses of juice and coffee. She offered them to us. We decided to have a cup of coffee. She invited us to her office while her two employees were out front. "So are you guys having a good time? We've been praying for you guys," Lola said. "Who's we?" I asked. "The ladies in my prayer group." Again, Rachel said, "Wow! Thank you for that. I guess God really does love us no matter what." Lola smiled and said, "Of course, he does. Will we be seeing you guys tomorrow? I'd love to introduce you to the ladies. But if you can't make it, just know you're loved by us and we're here praying for you all as God leads us to." Rachel and I looked at each other, and we both said, "We'll be there!" We laughed, and I said, "Now let's get out here and spend some money and bless this warrior of God." We each bought two outfits. One of them was for my mother as a way of thanking her for taking care of the children during the week. We went to get some food after we left the boutique because my appetite had returned.

We went back to the resort, and there was Fritz doing his thing, greeting those coming and going and making sure everyone was comfortable. As we waited for the elevator, Rachel and I talked about how unbelievable the day had been so far. We concluded that God was definitely ordering our steps. The elevator doors opened, and there were London and David. They stepped off, and David was telling Rachel how he had been calling her all day. "I thought we had a connection, Rachel. Please don't do this to us." Rachel told him she couldn't believe anything he said anymore because he hid the fact that his friend was married. She told him, "Obviously, you don't support the constitution of marriage, and that tells me a lot about your true character. Besides, I realize I deserve better for myself. How do I know you're not married? David, please stop calling me. It's over." London looked at me, shook his head, and walked right by me, saying nothing. Thank God because I had nothing to say to him. They walked over to the others in their group and began checking out as they had a late flight back to California, which was two hours behind the Florida time zone. We got on the elevator, and as the doors began to close, we saw Fritz talking to them. Rachel and I looked at each other, and then she said, "Oh, to be a fly on that wall over there!" I smiled and said, "No, thank you, I'm good right here."

When we got to the room and put our things away, Rachel said, "Trish, I've been thinking about the events of this trip. There's so much I could say, but I'll say this. I can see the sermon that Pastor preached before we left being played out right before us. We spoke into existence the Stella scenes from the movie. We saw God's grace and his mercy in action when we repented. And he sent his people to pray for us, and we didn't even know it. Wow, if that ain't love, I don't know what it is. This trip has turned out to be a trip where I can see that scripture come to light. I don't exactly know how it goes, but it says something like 'What the devil meant for evil, God turned it around for our good.'" "Yep, Rach, you're right. I never thought about it like that, but that's exactly right! I asked God to help me forgive London because you know who he made me think of, don't you?" Rachel looked at me and said, "Your ex! I'm not saying his name 'cause I promised you I wouldn't say his name while we are on this trip." "Thank you for that, and yes, that's who! You know, Rach, I used to wonder what the big deal was about struggling to be celibate. I understand now and feel more compassionate toward singles in that area now. Forgive me, Lord, for judging them. I see how a person can get caught up in it once you open that door." We just sat there, thinking for a moment. Then I broke the silence by saying, "And that, Fritz, can you believe that? I'm speechless about him, but I'm so grateful to God for putting him in our lives." Rachel smiled and said yeah. We decided to do something for him before we left, so we went back out to get him and his sister gifts to express our gratitude.

The rest of our time there in Florida, we woke up mornings and had devotions, and before we went to bed, we prayed. We did go to church the next day, and to our surprise, the greeter escorted us to the front row to be seated next to Lola. The presence of the Lord could be felt in that place. The people were so friendly and so filled with joy. They kind of made us think of the way Fritz was when we first met him. Neither Rachel nor I had ever been in a predominantly white church; not that it makes a difference because love is clear. We gave Lola her gift and thanked her for everything as we sat down. Just then, the worship team began to sing, and the anointing filled the place. I got weak in the knees when Rachel elbowed me and told me to look over there, and when I did, Fritz was there walking up the steps which led to the podium. He chuckled as he saw us with our mouths hanging open. Fritz was the pastor! Rachel leaned over to me and said in her joking voice, "Oooooh, girl, God's gonna get you for lusting after the pastor." I couldn't even respond. He introduced the speaker, who was so powerful, and both Rachel and I went up to the altar for prayer, and the Holy Spirit was all over us. We both got filled with the Holy Spirit, and we felt like we were being washed from the inside out. This whole experience changed our lives forever!

After the service, Lola introduced us to the prayer team that prayed for us. One of the ladies said she felt such a heaviness and urgency for us, so they prayed until they felt a release. Rachel said, "I can't believe you'd do that for people you don't even know." At that moment, Fritz walked up and said, "We don't have to know you; God does. We just have to be available to be used by him.

There's no love that can be compared to his love," as he pointed up. I was frozen and could not speak for a moment. So Rachel said, "You're the pastor of this church?" "Yes, I am. And I know your next question. Why am I working at the resort, right?" I shook my head up and down. Lola explained that their parents owned the resort and Fritz manages it. That made so much sense as to why he always seemed to be there and was just so knowledgeable of everything. They had refreshments in the back, and that was where we met Lola and Fritz's parents. What an incredible day. What an incredible trip! This is definitely one I'll never forget nor do I want to forget.

Fritz later told me just before we left that God laid me on his heart from the moment he first saw me and he had been praying for me since. "Sometimes we never know how God is going to use us, but we do know it's for a purpose. I don't know why he gave me a special connection to you, but his will be done." I was so messed up by the events of the whole day, but especially this evening. "Fritz," I said, "I feel so bad." He wanted to know why and about what. I told him about the real estate guys. Well . . . not everything. He stopped me and said he already knew. He said God told him these guys were being used by the enemy to block us from what God had for us and he was to intercede for us. When he told Lola, she told him God told her the same thing, so they all interceded on our behalf. "Trish, I know you've been hurt deeply, and God showed me you had an issue with trusting again. I'd been praying for that too." I replied, "That's amazing because at the altar this evening, I felt in my heart God telling me to give that to him, and in exchange, he would give me renewed trust. I gave it to him. You know, my ex-husband betrayed me, and I always kept a brick wall around my heart ever since then." At that point, Rachel came to me and asked if I was ready for her to call for the van. Fritz said he'd take us back.

So after exchanging numbers and social media info, we said

our goodbyes to our new friends and left with Fritz, who took us back to the resort. Rachel thanked him and went up to the room. "Fritz, I just don't know how to thank you. The gift we brought you just doesn't seem adequate enough." He took my hand and said, "It doesn't end here, Trish. I'd like to get to know you on a more personal level, but not now. Let's just be friends and truly get to know each other and see what the Lord does here. Are you okay with that?" I suddenly felt so much peace come over me, almost like God was saying a big *yes*! I agreed, and we went to my room.

The remainder of our trip was absolutely fantastic. Rachel decided to be celibate 'til she got married, and I renewed that promise to God. When we got home, the first thing Greg said to me was, "You look different!! What happened to you? You look so peaceful. I think I need to take a trip too if it's gonna do that for me!" I smiled and told him if he did decide to take a trip, I recommended he go to the same place we went to because it does wonders for the body, soul, and spirit.

Well, that's the end of my story, Rachel and I have never been the same, and we both kept our promise to God. She is now married to a wonderful man who treats her like the queen she is. Greg and one of his buddies did take that same trip, and Fritz and his church accepted them with open arms and changed their lives too. And me . . . I'm still not married and still celibate. It's been a year since our trip to the Panhandle, and Fritz and I talk often. He's been here twice to visit, and I've been back there twice. I've learned to watch my words because they are powerful. No more Stella talk or judging before I understand. I use my words to build people up and tear the enemy's kingdom down. It's a beautiful thing when you do it God's way.

Some Things Are Worth Holding On To

With God all things are possible.
Matthew 19:26

I remember when I was a boy, my Pops used to be out in his shed, tinkering around on things, building or repairing something. He was the greatest man alive; he was my hero. He was so smart and could calculate anything. I remember he used to say, "Who needs a calculator? My calculator is right here!" while pointing at his head. He taught us to do the same. He would tell me, my sister, and my little brother; "Nothing is hard. You just have to figure out how it works and work it." That way of thinking has helped me in many ways over the years. But I don't want to get ahead of my story. First, let me introduce myself. My name is Andre Portugal. I was born in a small country town in Louisiana, but we moved from there to San Diego, California, when I was twelve years old. This was a big culture shock to me because we lived in a small country town where everybody knew everybody, a town where there were no secrets, at least not with Ms. Ethel around; that lady knew everybody's business. Some folks swore she had microphones in each house. Our town had one church, one small hospital, one jail, one bank, one high school, and one elementary school. We were a community, but we were also like a family. It was hard moving, especially to Mom. This was where all her friends were, and she was pretty popular, a role model, some might say, to the other ladies. Pops got a job in San Diego because of something he invented. We kids didn't realize it at the time, but our pops had just become a millionaire for one of his tinkerings.

Culture Shock

I'll never forget the day we finally got into San Diego. We drove from Louisiana, and that was the longest trip we had ever taken by car. I was twelve, my sister was ten, and my brother was eight, so you can imagine what that was like. I was mesmerized, with my face glued to the window, as we drove past the downtown skyline. Little did I know that my life was about to change forever. We went from slow and steady to fast and impetuous. There were so many buildings, and they were so tall. I had never seen so many people, cars, and trucks all at the same time.

We turned on to a winding lane that was beautifully traced with white stones along the road, and the grass was so green and neat. We approached the house, and I wanted to know who lived in that big house. My mother told us it was our house. We were shocked. You see we had just come from a small three-bedroom house. Well, it was really a two-bedroom house, but Mom converted the dining room into a third bedroom. It had one bathroom and a nice big porch on the back of the house, which was my favorite place. It was screened in and had a door. Whenever we couldn't go outside and play because of the weather, we'd play on that porch. Pops had invented something to cover the screens by just pushing a button and some type of clear plastic would cover them. He was so smart. A lot of the kids would come over and play when it would rain because of that.

Apparently, it was that invention that landed us in San Diego.

Forgiving Is Easy . . . Or Is It

One of our neighbors back in Louisiana, the Fosters, had a relative come visit them from Cali. While they were there, all the kids had come over to our house to play on the back porch because it was raining outside. That relative, Mr. Banks, asked why the kids all played at our house when it rained, and when he was told, he immediately wanted to meet my Pops. One thing led to another, and here we are in Cali. I didn't understand all that legal stuff I heard Mom and Pops talking about, but I did hear them say it was the hand of God that gave them true and honest people to help them. One thing about Mom, no matter what was going on, she would pray about it. I saw my sister starting to act just like Mom, especially in that regard. She had gotten to the point that I hardly wanted to do anything around her cause she always wanted to pray about it. Thinking back on that now, I laugh because she would move and pace the floor while she prayed, just like Mom. This girl was only ten years old.

Before we got out of the car, Pops said, laughing, "Okay, y'all, your mama's gonna pray over us and the house before we go in. When we go inside, y'all can go through the house and explore. There are four bedrooms upstairs. We've already picked out who would be in which one, but y'all can go through and pick the one you want and we'll see if it matches what we've picked out for you." Mom couldn't get finished fast enough with her praying. As soon as she said amen, we burst out the doors and ran around the house, checking out the backyards, and discovered we had another big screened-in porch with a door; only this porch was even bigger. Pops had his invention put on the house, both in the front and back porches. We also had a pool. A big pool and a pool house. Mom said everybody in California has a pool. Good thing we all knew how to swim.

We went inside and paused at the front door because it was so big inside. Our mouths were hanging open. It felt like a dream. Pops was standing at the top of the stairs, laughing at us, and said,

"Come on up here and pick your rooms!" Before he could finish that sentence, I bolted up the stairs, with my sister, Jenny, and my brother, Jerry, not far behind. We had so much fun. It felt like more fun than I could take. Looking back on it now, I realized I was just overwhelmed. The rooms we picked out turned out to be the same ones Pops said they picked out for us. Years later, we learned that they really hadn't picked out any rooms for us; they said that so we wouldn't fight over the rooms. Jenny's room suited her because there was a built-in bookcase in the wall. Lord knows that girl loves to read, even to this day. That's why she's so smart too. Jerry's room had a small section off to the side where he put all his Lego stuff. He was a tinker too, only with Legos. And my room, of course, was the best! It had a bigger space off to the side of it where I put a desk and all my projects. You see, I liked to build things. I had a solar system I created using wire, Styrofoam paint, and clay. It was so cool. I hung it in my room. I also built a volcano that actually worked. Whatever I could think of, I'd try to create it. After all, Pops taught us to calculate in our heads and to figure out how things work and then work it. Seeing how big that space was off my room made me not want to wait to unpack; I wanted to start building right away! Okay, okay, I guess you could say we were nerdy, but we were cool nerds.

The fourth room was Pop's room. He called it his thinking room. We were only allowed there if we were called there because he had his thinking stuff in there, and it was a lot. Mom had her own room too, which she called her prayer room. You can guess what went on in there, and believe me, there was *a lot* going on in there too. The master bedroom was on the first floor, and it was so big. I heard Pops tell Mom he could chase her around the room now, and she giggled. All I thought was grown-ups were weird.

We all had so much fun shopping for our rooms. For me, it was simply a bed, dresser, and building stuff. Lots of it. Jerry was the same; his focus was on the space off his room. Legos and other building stuff made him happy. We were like Pops in that way. Now Jenny, that's another story. She really wanted to decorate her room. She and Mom went shopping for her because the first time Jerry and I went with them, we were bored out of our minds. All that girly stuff, who needs it. Mom didn't let her go overboard just because we had the money now; she truly wanted to keep us grounded, and she did. This was turning out to be the best summer we had ever had. We had another month before we went to school. Fortunately, we met some kids at our new church during that month, which made going to school not so bad because we already know some of the kids.

We all made great grades because we read a lot and Pops would always ask us questions about what we read. Mom would give an assignment once a week during the summer, and then we were tested on it. She didn't believe in us doing nothing, and if you said you were bored, she would surely find something for you to do. We all seemed to be doing well in school, but the bigness of it all was so overwhelming. Pops got Jerry and I involved with a group of boys through his company, where we did experiments and built things. We both loved it, especially because it was a small group of six boys. Jenny, on the other hand, wasn't having such a great time. The girls were not being nice to her, she said. Mom would spend time with her, talking about things and praying with her. Eventually, things got better, and though it was a shock culturally, we got through it pretty good.

Discovery

As time went by, I entered high school. This was where things began to really change for me. I guess I started feeling myself. Looking back on it, I really made some dumb decisions. As smart as I was, I started hanging out with the crowd Mom told me to avoid. I couldn't take the pressure of being "different," as they said.

So I was determined to prove them wrong. I decided to try my hand at sports and discovered I was pretty good. I tried out for the baseball team and got on as a second baseman/shortstop. I was so good that during my sophomore year, I played varsity instead of JV (junior varsity). Not only did the coaches notice me, so did the girls. I never thought much of myself until they started smiling and waving at me. Some also gave me their numbers, and I didn't even ask for them. My new friends told me I had to "hit some of that." I went along with it 'cause I didn't want them to know I had never "hit it" before. The locker room talk was about sports and girls. I felt kind of bad for some of the girls they were talking about because it wasn't anything nice. Our team captain and my friend, Troy, told us this one girl, Melissa, was really easy to hit. He said, laughing, "Man, I broke her in. She was a virgin. She's real easy. Just give her a little attention and tell her you're into her and she'll give it up. But I'm telling you, don't tell her you love her or you'll have a stalker on your hands. Hit it and then just blow her off." Our teammate Ronnie said, "Man, I bet I can get more numbers than you at Q's party Friday night." So the guys agreed to see which one could come back with the most numbers. Next was to see how many girls they could hit from those numbers. If they hit, they had to prove it by somehow taking a picture of her bra with her in the picture. The guys called me Li'l Man 'cause I was only a sophomore. Troy told me he would teach me anything I wanted to know. He was the only one, I thought, that knew I was still a virgin.

Mom and Pops didn't like the changes they saw in me, but Pops told Mom it's different with boys than girls. He told her, "Baby, the pressure to have sex is real strong, especially when you are as popular as Andre is. I know the boys are not letting up on him and will probably use him to get girls. He's popular and good looking; the girls will automatically come around him and whoever he's with." My mom was concerned about me, but

Pops told her I would be all right. He reminded her, "You know you always say ain't nothing too hard for the Lord." Those words made Mom feel better, and she asked Pops to pray with her for me, and he did.

Our team had to go to Arizona to play in a tournament. We were up against one of the toughest teams we had played so far. Before we left, Pops told me he wanted to talk to me, so we went out and sat by the pool. He said, "Andre, I want you to know how proud I am of you and all your accomplishments. You remind me of myself when I was your age. Now I know you haven't come to me to talk about these girls that are coming at you, so I'm coming to you." I looked at him in surprise and said, "How do you know they are coming around me?" He laughed and said, "Like I said, you remind me of me when I was your age; only I was better looking." He stroked his goatee. I said, "Yeah, yeah, keep dreaming, Pops!" We both laughed at that point. Then he said, "Son, your mom and I want you to know we've been praying for you. I know what it's like. I wasn't playing sports, but the girls always came around because of my hazel eyes and dimples; at least that's what they used to always talk about. You got them too, but you didn't get the chin dimple. Oh, and by the way, that's how I hooked your mother! She just couldn't and still can't resist these eyes and dimples." I laughed and said, "Thanks, Pops! So you're to blame for these girls dropping their phone numbers on me. I ain't complaining, but sometimes it's hard when the fellows start talking." Pops asked me directly, "Have you had sex?" "No, sir, I haven't. You know, Pops, sometimes it gets real hard 'cause some of these girls are so bold. One girl came and sat next to me and put her hand on my thigh and squeezed it; I didn't know what to do. The fellows trash-talk the girls real bad in the locker. Troy is the only one that knows I haven't had sex, and sometimes I get scared that they'll ask me if I have or not. I don't want to lie, but I don't want to look like a punk either." Pops looked at me and asked, "Son, do you still pray and read your Bible?" I held my head down and said, "Well, no, sir, not really."

Pops put his hand on my shoulder and said, "You might want to start there. Don't forget, you're never alone. God said he would never leave you or forsake you. This is not the first time he's had to deal with something like this. Son, he is the way of escape. Just talk to him. He's always with you. Promise me you'll do that." I looked at him with tears in my eyes and said, "I will, Pops. Thanks." He extended his hand to me, and I shook it and pulled him to me, hugged him, and said in his ear, "You're still my hero, Pops."

The next morning, I got up a little early and read my Bible and prayed. I have to admit, it seemed strange; I don't really know when I had stopped. Then I got myself together, had breakfast, and went over to Mom, who was in her prayer room. I knocked on her open door. She looked up and smiled and motioned for me to come in. "Morning, Mom," I said and kissed her on her cheek. She looked at me and smiled and stroked the side of my face and said, "Dre, I'm so proud to be your mother, and I want you to know I believe in you. Be safe, make wise choices, and win!" "Okay," I said with a smile.

I felt a newfound strength, like I could conquer the world. In fact, the whole team was hyped. There was so much energy on that bus. The coaches were giving us motivational speeches, along with our team captain, Troy. We were excited and ready to kick butt! Needless to say, we did just that, and I scored the winning runs for the last two games we played! The energy was even more intense on winning all the games. We didn't lose a single game. We were the champs! To celebrate, there was a party thrown in our honor. Alcohol was not allowed, but a couple of guys snuck some in. There were girls everywhere, and I meant everywhere. I tried to duck out when some of the guys grabbed me and said, "Here's our champ, Lil' Man! We got a surprise for you." They escorted me to one of the rooms and pushed me in and said have fun. "You're going in a boy but coming out a man!" Then they all laughed as they closed the door and locked it from their side. I saw a very pretty girl sitting on a chair in the room. I froze. I could hear my heart beating and feel it pounding in my chest. The guys knew I was still a virgin, and this was their way of "helping me out." I guess the girl could tell I was nervous and scared because she came over, took my hand, and told me to relax. She said I looked scared and tense. "I promise I won't bite you," she said. She led me over to the bed, and we sat down. She put her hand on my knee while telling me I played a great game. She asked my name as she slowly began to move her hand up my thigh. I grabbed her hand and sharply asked her what she was doing. She looked shocked and said, "I'm sorry! I'm sorry!" I looked at her and saw I scared her with the tone of my voice, but she caught me off guard. She tried to make the moment mellow by saying, "You're really good. I mean you're a real good ball player. How'd you get so good?" "I don't know. It just comes naturally," I said. "I didn't even know I could play. I've always been interested in building things and never even played sports seriously until last year." She looked surprised and said, "Really? I know this is going to sound strange, but I like to build things too. It's kind of a passion, I guess." She put her head down and said, "I know that sounds nerdy." I quickly said, "No, it doesn't. I come from a family that likes to build things." Then I told her about how we came to San Diego. She was so impressed and said, "I know who you are now! My father is the one that got your father the deal and job here. He told us about his invention, and we have it on our front and back porches. This is amazing! By the way, my name is Kaitlyn Banks. I'm sorry for what I did to you. Your team wanted to do something special for you and thought this would be a good idea. They said you're a virgin and wanted me to seduce you. I feel so ashamed. Please forgive me." She lowered her head. I said, "Well, Kaitlyn, I don't know what you're talking about 'cause that never happened, so let's just start over." I extended my hand to her and shook her hand and said, "My name is Andre Portugal, and it's nice to meet a fellow undercover nerd." We both laughed.

I shared with Kaitlyn about all the things I had built and told her about the program Jerry and I were in through Pop's job. She said she knew all about that program because she wanted to be in it, but it was only for boys. She shared with me the things she built, and I couldn't believe it. I asked her if I could see them, and she said, "Sure!" I was amazed at the way she spoke of the things she built. She seemed like a different person when she talked about her passion. She knew the language of a builder, and it sounded like she was a great one. I couldn't wait to see what she built. "I don't think this is what the fellows had in mind when they locked that door," I said. "Yeah, I know," Kaitlyn said. So we spent the time in that room getting to know each other. Then we heard the door being unlocked and opened. The fellows started shouting and pumping their fists in the air. Ronnie said, "We're going to have to call Lil' Man Big Man now!" They grabbed me and put me in a headlock and said how proud of me they were. I never told them what actually happened, and neither did Kaitlyn.

We were all proud of our trophies and the big team trophy, which was put in the showcase display at school. We were the champs! When we were headed back to San Diego on the bus, while most everyone was sleeping, I was awake and thinking and thanking God for working it out. I realized what Mom said was true, "prayer works." Of course, the guys wanted to know the details, but I played it off and said I don't kiss and tell. Troy looked at me and winked his eye.

When we got back, Kaitlyn was already there, and she was among those waiting for us. I saw her before I got off the bus and smiled. Troy looked at me and said, "Yeah, yeah, man! I saw that. What really happened in there with y'all?" I looked at him and gave him a fist bump and said, "You'll never know." He smiled and said, "Ahhh, that's cool, man, but you know I know you didn't hit that. You know what, Lil' Man, you all right with me!" He said this as he put his arm around my neck and bumped me in the top of my head with his fist.

When I got off the bus, I saw Pops and Jerry waiting for me by the car. I was walking toward them when Kaitlyn called out to me. I turned, and she ran up to me and said, "Would you like to come over sometime and see the things I built?" "Yeah, I'd like that, Kaitlyn. How 'bout tomorrow?" I said. She was cool with that, and before she turned and walked away, she kissed me on the cheek and said, "Dre, you really are one of the good ones." Of course, I blushed, and then she said, "I love those dimples!"

While I was approaching the car, Pops and Jerry were smiling at me. Then Jerry said, "Who was that? Bro, she's pretty." I said she was just a friend, but Pops gave me a look that said yeah right! On the way home, we talked all about the games and the victories. I was so tired and just wanted to rest, especially since I was going to Kaitlyn's tomorrow. Jenny and Mom were waiting at home with a small victory celebration. It was so nice being home again, but I must admit, I was still kind of hyped up mentally, but I think this time, it was because of Kaitlyn. I was in the kitchen getting some juice, and Mom came in and asked, "How did it go?" I said it was great and told her I couldn't believe all the attention I got for scoring the winning runs for the last two games. She smiled and said, "That's my Dre!" I could tell she was so happy. Then Pops came in and said, "Son, let's take a walk." So we went out and walked around the trail we had behind our house.

All About Kaitlyn

"So who's the young lady that kissed you? I know you didn't tell your mama about her." I told Pops how the guys set me up with Kaitlyn because somehow they found out I was still a virgin. Pops said, "Okay now, you did say 'still a virgin,' right?" "Yeah, Pops, I am." As I told him everything that happened, he smiled and nodded his head. "You know, your mama felt like something was going on and asked me to join her in prayer for you. I sho do appreciate that woman. She definitely has a connection with God." Then I told him what she said about her father being the one responsible for us being in California. Pops said, "Wait a minute, that's Joe Banks's daughter?" I said, "I guess so. Her last name is Banks, and get this, Pops, she loves to build things!" I told him all about the things she told me she built and that I was going over to her house tomorrow to see them. "I guess you'll meet Joe too then. Son, he's a real good man. God gave us somebody that is fair in business, and I'm grateful. You know, I didn't know anything about the business side of things. I just loved to build things. Once again, your mama prayed for the right people to help us with all this, and Joe truly was an answered prayer. That brother is just as quick at business and contracts as I am about building and calculating." Then Pops gave me a serious look and said, "Dre, be gentle with his daughter because something must be wrong for her to sell herself short to try and seduce you." "Yeah, Pops, I already thought about that. Actually, I prayed about it." Pops looked at me with a huge grin on his face. "That's my boy! Treat her like the lady she is, not the seductress female she's not. You never know what happened in her life to make her settle for that." We bumped fists and headed home. Of course, Jerry wanted to know all about her, so I told him I was going over to her house tomorrow and I would tell him more after that. One thing I did tell him was that she was a builder too. He said he never heard of a girl builder before and said he thought it was real cool.

When I went to Kaitlyn's house the next day, I was amazed; their house was awesome. I saw Pop's invention on the front porch covering the screen. I was so proud of him. This was the first time

I actually saw one of his inventions being used by someone other than family. I rang the bell, and her father came to the door. I knew he was her father because he looked like her. "Hello, you must be Andre Portugal, Anthony's son." I felt a bit nervous and said, "Yes, sir, I am." He shook my hand and told me to come in. Their house was big too, and they had a pool as well. Mom did say everybody in Cali has a pool. I met Kaitlyn's mother; her two sisters, Jill and Kelly; and her two brothers, Joe Jr. and Marvin. Both of her brothers were older than me, and they seemed really cool.

I went into a tailspin when she took me to this room where she did her building. It was as if everything else disappeared. I felt at home. Suddenly, looking at all her projects made baseball take a back seat. My love and passion for building was coming back like never before. This girl was . . . well, there was no other word for it; she was simply amazing. Mr. Banks knocked on the door and came in and affirmed that she had indeed built all these projects. He walked next to her and put his arm around her and was beaming with pride. He spoke with us for a moment, and then her mother came in with a snack for us and invited me to stay for dinner. "I'd love that!" I said happily.

The Price of Innocence

Kaitlyn and I talked about building for about the next hour and a half. Then I said to her, "There's something I've been wondering. I hope you don't mind me asking this, but why were you the one the team picked to seduce me?" She became really quiet, so I said, "You don't have to answer that if you don't want to." She said, "No, it's all right. I was trying to fit in with the cool girls. When I was in junior high, building wasn't cool anymore if I wanted to be popular. The pressure was really bad when I got in high school. They started calling me a nerd my freshman year. The cool girls told me I had the looks and if I wanted to hang with them, I had to stop acting like a nerd or geek. There was this party one of the juniors was having, and my new friends told me if I wanted to be cool, I had to lose my virginity and gain respect. I was so desperate not to be teased like they did my old best friend from elementary school. She and I used to build together; only she didn't care about being popular. I, on the other hand, did. I made the terrible decision to follow the crowd and lost something I can never get back. You know, Dre, what's really sad, that guy doesn't even look at me anymore. He could care less about me. It was a horrible experience. I didn't like it and decided I didn't want to go through with it because he was hurting me. I told him to stop, but he wouldn't." As I looked at Kaitlyn, she looked like she wanted to cry. At that point, I found myself getting mad; the more she told me, the angrier I got. She continued, "He'd been drinking, and I could tell he was kinda drunk. I couldn't stop him. When he was done, he just got up, got himself together, and walked out. I wanted so badly to be popular and cool. I just kept a certain look and pretended to be okay. I thought that was the way it was supposed to be." I asked if the guy went to our school, and she said yes. Things were quiet for a moment, and then she said, "You know him. He's on your team. I had to make it with a popular guy so I could be popular. It was Troy." Just then, I remembered how bad he talked about Melissa and wondered if he had done that about Kaitlyn. I wanted to know if she had been with any of the other guys, but then again, I didn't. I didn't know what to say, so I didn't say anything. My mind was filled with all kinds of thoughts. Troy was my friend, but I didn't want him as my friend anymore. I wondered if that was why he wanted to know what really happened in that room. Then one of her sisters, Jill, came and told us to come eat. I enjoyed being with her family; it took the edge off. Her brothers were cool dudes. Joe Jr. was in college, playing football, and he came home this weekend to visit. Her other brother, Marvin, was a senior in high school and said he was going to be an architect. These guys were some big dudes, and they both looked like they played football. If Kaitlyn had told them what Troy did, I'm sure they would have crushed him. Her sister Jill was a junior, and her younger sister, Kelly, was a freshman. Kaitlyn was a sophomore.

After dinner, Kaitlyn and I went for a walk. She asked me if I was mad at her. "Of course not!" I said. "I guess I was just shocked because Troy was my friend, but not anymore. I won't be friends with anyone that hurt you like that." Kaitlyn smiled warmly and said, "And in case you're wondering if I've been with any of the other guys on the team, the answer is no. I was just going through the motions so I would be seen as popular. Troy told me to do that with you, or he would show the pictures he said he had of me nude. To be honest, that was my first and last time. It just didn't feel right. So you see, Andre, I was actually just as scared and nervous as you were. Dre, why didn't you make any moves on me at the party?" Okay, I knew it was now or never to tell her I was a Christian. I took a deep breath and said, "I'm a Christian, Kaitlyn. I got saved when I was in the eighth grade, but I've been in church all my life. I understand the pressure you felt to fit in. I went through that too when I got on the baseball team, but my parents kept me grounded and levelheaded. All that popularity I suddenly had was beginning to change me, but my mother . . .," I said with a smile on my face, "she is a prayer warrior and prays for all her children like there's no tomorrow." I laughed. Kaitlyn had a funny look on her face and said, "Wow, I never heard of anything like that. You're lucky. My parents are great, but they don't do anything like that!" Then she was quiet for a moment and said, "Dre, do you pray?" I told her I recently started back. I told her that when I got on the team, at some point, I stopped praying and reading my Bible. She looked shocked and said, "You read the Bible too?" "Yeah, I did and just recently started back.

Kaitlyn, reading the Bible helps me a lot. Mom got us Bibles that were easy for us to understand 'cause we just didn't get all those *thees* and *thous*. I didn't want the guys to know, so I basically kept it to myself." We went over to sit on a bench under a big tree. We both were quiet for about three minutes. Kaitlyn was so curious and wanted to know more. She said, "So exactly what does it mean to be saved? Saved from what?" I began to tell her about the love of God, and I explained John 3:16 to her.

"For God so loved the world that he gave his only begotten son, that whoever believes in him should not die but have life eternally." She asked questions, and I was silently asking God to give me the answers. She said, "I feel funny, kinda like I need to be saved too. How do I get saved?" So right there on that bench, under that big tree, I led Kaitlyn to the Lord. This was a first for me. She cried and cried. I didn't know what to do, so I just let her. Then she said, "I feel so clean inside. Can you ask your mother what's a good Bible for me to read so I can understand it too." "Sure," I said. "In fact, let me call her now and see what she recommends and we can go get one now, if you want." "Yeah, I love that!" she said.

Mom was so excited and started praising God right on the phone. Pops ended up taking the phone from her because, as he said, "Son, I don't know what you told yo mama, but she's on a totally different level now! She's outta there with the Lord." So I told him, and he was so happy to hear the news too. He made some suggestions to me and told me to just let her browse through some of the Bibles and let her pick her own. God will guide her." Pops was always my man; he came through again. I didn't even get to ask Mom about which Bible to get because as soon as she heard I led Kaitlyn to the Lord, she went off!

Kaitlyn told me while we were at the bookstore looking through the Bibles that she felt like she was floating on air. She said she didn't know any other way to describe how she felt. We found a great Bible for her, and she loved it. It was a study Bible, one especially for teen girls. Just looking at Kaitlyn, I could see a different person. She looked so, so, well . . . not just happy, but joyful. After we left the bookstore, I took her to see my mom 'cause I knew if I didn't, I wouldn't hear the last of it. Mom hugged Kaitlyn so tight and took her into her prayer room. I guess to tell her some basics. Thirty minutes later, they came out talking and giggling like old friends.

And Now

Kaitlyn and I became really good friends. Well, actually, she became my girlfriend. We had fun growing in the Lord and building projects together. Jerry even joined us on a couple of them. We entered some of them in contests and won everything. I never knew a girl like Kaitlyn before. Baseball was still a fun sport, and I did finish out playing my sophomore and junior year, but during my senior year, I got more serious about my future, and I knew it wasn't in baseball. That to me now was a hobby. I graduated high school with honors and went on to college and, yup, you guessed it, married Kaitlyn. As it turned out, Troy never had any pictures of Kaitlyn. It was something the guys said to control young, naive girls. I know it's probably hard to believe, but we didn't have sex until we got married. Sometimes it was hard, but because we were working toward the same goal, that made it easier.

And now here we are reminiscing with old high school friends who came together at our twenty-year reunion. Troy was there with his wife, and when Kaitlyn saw him, she said it was at that moment that she knew she had truly forgiven him for doing what he did and for lying by saying he had pictures. Kaitlyn and I have three very smart boys. We are very successful and help other families who are less fortunate. And yes, we still work on projects together and include the kids too.

One day, Pops came over with Mom. After playing with the

kids, Mom was in the kitchen with Kaitlyn, and Pops and I sat out by the pool, chilling. I said, "Pops, I remember when we lived in Louisiana and if we wanted to know anything, we could ask Ms. Ethel." Pops laughed and said, "Yup, sure could. That woman knew everybody's business. You and Mom taught us not to rely on the gossip but to talk to God ourselves. I never dreamed back then that those words would be so powerful in my life. You also told us to take our time and figure out how something works and then work it. I think that's why I was so good at baseball. I studied the swing, pitch, distance between the bases, and how to use the wind to help me if it were a windy day. You never ever seemed to get tired of us when we were little and full of questions. Pops, I just want to say thanks. All those things have helped me to be a good father to my boys. I don't ever remember you blowing us off, but you listened to us and looked out for Mom all the time. I appreciate you, and guess what?" I noticed Pops wiping his eyes and taking his hanky and blowing his nose. Pops said weakly, trying not to cry, "Boy, you don't have to say all that stuff. I know how you feel." I told him, "Yeah, but I want you to hear me say it even in my thirties. Pops, you're still my hero!" I hugged him, and he cried. Then through his tears, he said, "Dre, I'm proud of you. You're my hero too."

Who Would've Known

You did not choose me, but I chose you and appointed you so that you might go and bear fruit—fruit that will last—and so that whatever you ask in my name the Father will give you.
John 15:16 NIV

Frank and I have been married for six happy years. There were moments of awkwardness at the beginning because we were getting to know each other as husband and wife. We don't have any children yet for some reason, but we're still happy with just us. You see, we live in a beautiful neighborhood with lots of children, and we have lots of nieces and nephews, so they basically are our children. The best part is we get to send them home whenever we want to. I have a great job as a high fashion designer, and my husband is a security guard at a bank. Yeah, I know, what a combination. I'm not really sure what drew us together because we are so different. He said he was attracted to my looks, meaning the shape of my body, and my style. I love looking good; I always dress to impress. I'm very social, up-front, and friendly. He, on the other hand, is fine wearing a T-shirt and jeans. His idea of dressing up is a polo shirt and khaki pants with loafers or sneakers. At least he prefers his sneakers to be a name brand. Don't get me wrong, there's nothing wrong with that look. But to me, that's casual. However, it suits his personality, and I love him. Frank is very laid-back, reserved, and passive. Too passive for me, and that's one of the things that secretly bothers me. I don't feel like he'd ever fight for me if the need ever came up. Now fighting with me he has no problem with; he talks tough to me, but no one else. But even then that's rare. For the most part, I like our life.

Strange

One day, I came home early, and while driving up our street, I noticed from a distance a car parked across the street in front of our house. Of course, I was curious because Frank was at work, so I wondered. Most of the people on our block were at work, so there were no cars parked on the street, which made this car stand out even more. We all had driveways, but even they were empty during the day. As I drove up slowly, I decided to park at a distance and observe. A few minutes later, I noticed a man walking to the car from our house. As he got to his car, he turned with a camera in his hand and took some pictures of our house, got in his car, and drove off. That was strange, I thought; he only took pictures of our house.

When Frank got home, I told him about it, and he reminded me of the neighborhood watch. I had completely forgotten about them because our neighborhood is so quiet and not much happens 'til the weekends. In our area, each block had a camera, which we protested about when they first installed them, but then again, nothing ever happens in our affluent neighborhood. So Frank said he'd check with the security office and see what turns up. Thank God, I thought, because he is usually so passive about things and just blows them off, but I guess seeing how concerned I was made him take action. He also said it could be a realtor company taking pictures of the houses because they did that periodically. Nevertheless, he kissed me on the cheek and said I didn't have anything to worry about. "By the way, sweetie," Frank said to me as he glared passionately at me walking away, "did I tell you how beautiful you look today?" I turned to him and blushed and said, "No, so tell me." He smiled and told me to keep walking because he was enjoying the view. "Frank," I said, giggling, "you're so silly."

The next day at work, I was working on designs for a big photo shoot we had coming up for a prestigious client when Bert knocked on my opened office door and asked if I wanted to go to lunch with them, and I said yes. I loved this time of year because the leaves were starting to change colors and the air was crisp. We were talking about the upcoming holidays when Kathy said, "Has anyone noticed that man at the bar? He keeps staring at us through the mirror. We turned to look, and when we did, he pulled down his hat and told the bartender he wanted to pay his bill. Ralph said, "That's strange. That looks like the same man I saw in the lobby at work. I noticed him because he was taking pictures. At that moment, I shared with them what happened the day before when I went home early. Bert said he'd alert security about it and tell them to keep an eye out. "So he likes taking pictures uh. He better not be trying to steal our designs." You see, it's not unusual for people to take pictures in our lobby because it was beautiful, but Ralph said that guy just kind of stood out. Bert said, "We'll find out who he is if he comes around again. Nothing gets past Rhonda!" Rhonda was the head of security, and she was sharp. That woman wasn't afraid of anything. She always says, "I'm protected by the blood of Jesus!" Plus, Bert had a crush on her anyway, and I think she had one on him too.

When I got home, Frank told me he'd spoken to our security people, and they said they would check the footage from the camera and get back to him tomorrow. I told him about the man at the bar watching us and what Ralph said. Frank took my hand and said, "Sweetie, I don't think we have anything to worry about. Our security people are on it, and Rhonda is one tough cookie." He knew Rhonda from high school. They grew up together, and she was the one who helped him get into security. Frank is passive, but my baby knows his stuff; he learned from Rhonda. He asked me if I wanted to go out for a drive and look at the beautiful trees because the leaves were changing colors. "Sure," I said. So after dinner, we did just that. We drove to the lookout point overlooking the Grove. I put hot apple cider in a thermos and brought two mugs, a blanket, and cushions to sit on. Frank backed into a spot at the Grove, and we got in the back of his truck and wrapped up in the blanket and drank hot apple cider. It was so relaxing as he played smooth jazz on the radio, and I must admit it took my mind off the bizarre recent events.

Love Is in the Air

The next day, when I got to work, I saw Bert and Rhonda talking in the lobby. He was standing in the doorway of the security office, talking to her. I went over to join them, and I said good morning. They both spoke, and Rhonda said, "Hey, Sabrina, Bert told me about what happened at your house the other day. I got this covered here. I saw the guy on our footage, but there is nothing strange or unusual about him. I can see his face, but not well. Don't worry, if he comes round again, we'll check him out. What's Frank doing about the guy who took pictures of your house?" I told her we should be hearing from our security people today about the footage they retrieved. She said she'd give Frank a call and see what he comes up with. As Bert and I left to go upstairs, I heard him ask Rhonda if she was free for lunch, and she said yes, so they decided to have lunch together. I caught a glimpse of her watching him as he was walking toward the elevator. She saw me, and I winked my eye at her, and she smiled. In the elevator, I asked Bert, "When are you going to make a move on Rhonda?" He said, "That's what lunch is, and why are you all in my business, Ms. Sabrina?" He was trying so hard not to smile. I told him she's a great person and he'd be a fool not to really get to know her. "She's real cool," I said. "She and Frank went to school together, and we've all hung out several times. She's got a good heart." Bert grinned and said, "That ain't all she got that's good." I looked at him and punched him in the arm and said, "Boy, get your mind out of the gutter." Bert said with a smile on his face, "There ain't nothing gutter about her. I think she's classy." I smiled and shook my head up and down and said, "You're right. You should see her outside of work. She really is classy." Bert said, "I plan to."

As I got into my day, I must admit I was so busy working on the designs that I forgot all about the strange man. That whole day was great. We were ahead of schedule with our designs and pretty much ready for the shoot. There were only a few last-minute details with the models, and we were set. Rhonda called me and asked if I'd heard anything from Frank yet. I told her no and when we did hear something, we'd let her know. When we left for the day, as I got off the elevator and was walking out with Kathy and Ralph, I couldn't shake the feeling of someone watching us. I looked around but saw nothing out of the ordinary. I looked over at the security office, and I saw Rhonda and Bert watching us. They waved, and we waved back.

Now That's Creepy

When I got home, Frank was already there with two of the security guys for our neighborhood. I spoke and kissed Frank and asked if everything was all right. The security guys, Benny and Kevin, were there to inform us they saw the guy on the footage and showed it to us. They got good shots of his face and asked if we recognized him. We told them we had never seen him before. Frank asked if he could possibly be a realtor. Kevin said, "No, they have to go through our security for clearance to do something like that, and we generally would ask you if you're okay with that. We'll keep an eye out and on all the surrounding streets as well. It may be nothing, but if something comes up with this, we'll handle it." So Frank walked them to the door, and they talked for a few minutes, and they left. Frank asked me if I was all right, and I told him yes. He held me, and I reminded him to call Rhonda and let her know what they found out.

The next few days were uneventful. Frank and I planned a barbecue at our house with a few friends, Rhonda, Bert, Ralph, Kathy, and a few of Frank's coworkers. We were having a great time when Frank got a call from Benny from the security gate. They spotted the man in the neighborhood again. Benny told Frank they were watching him and weren't sure how he got in, so they were going to track him and see how he leaves. Frank told Rhonda, and they went into full Rambo mode. I never saw my Frank like this before. Wow! Rhonda and Bert went across the street to watch the house from there. Frank and Ralph were watching from the house but trying to act normal just in case he was watching. Suddenly, I felt a bit scared. Kathy told me we're in good hands. "I wonder if it's the same man that was at work taking pictures," Kathy said. "If it is, now that's creepy," I said. Ten minutes later, they caught him snooping around the back of the house, trying to take pictures from a patch of trees. Frank called for Rhonda and Bert to come, and Benny and Kevin came with the guy in handcuffs. As soon as Rhonda saw him, she said, "That's the same man from work!" Frank ran up on the man and tried to grip him in his chest, but Benny stopped him. The man said, "I'm not trying to hurt anyone. If you look in my wallet, you'll see I'm a private investigator." Kevin checked, and sure enough, this man was telling the truth. They uncuffed him. He asked if he could speak to me in private. Before I could say anything, Frank said, "I'm going to pretend like you didn't just ask that stupid question."

So we went into my design room, Frank, myself, and the man. Rhonda told Frank to call out if he needed her.

The Truth Will Set You Free

So the man began his story. "My name is Mr. Willis of Willis & Brown Detective Agency. I was hired by a man who claims you're his daughter but wanted to know for sure before he approached you." I couldn't believe what I was hearing. Frank asked me if I was all right. I couldn't even say anything, so I just nodded. He continued, "He wants to reach out to you if you're okay with it. I think he should share the other details with you, but if you prefer, I will do so." I couldn't believe what I was hearing. My parents were my parents. They never gave a hint otherwise. I looked at him and said, "Is my mother my mother?" He told me, "No, they adopted you when you were two months old." I was devastated. I felt like my whole life was somehow a lie. So my brother and sisters were not really my brother and sisters? I didn't know what to believe. I burst out in tears. Rhonda knocked on the door and said, "Is everything all right in there?" Frank said, "Yes, I'll be out in a few minutes." Mr. Willis apologized for the hurt and confusion he caused. He left us information about my birth father and said he'd tell me about my birth mother. He said he didn't know much about her. Needless to say, the party was over. I went to my bedroom, and Frank saw everyone out. He thanked Benny and Kevin and everyone else. Rhonda told Frank, "If you need me, you know how to reach me. Frank, don't hesitate to call me. Sabrina is like a little sister to me. I'm praying for you both." After everyone left, Frank locked up and came to the room and found me lying on the bed, sobbing. He came over and didn't say a word. He just held me and let me cry. I felt so confused and had a thousand thoughts going through my mind. Eventually, Frank whispered to me, "Baby, you take as long as you need. I'm not going anywhere. I'm here for you." I fell asleep in his arms and woke up in his arms.

I felt like my life had ended, but I was still alive. I told Frank, "I have to confront Mama and Daddy, but I don't know what to say or how to say it. Will you come with me?" Frank took my hands in his and kissed them both and said, "There ain't no way I'm going to let you do that by yourself. I'm here, baby, all the way!" I couldn't even call them, so Frank did it for me and told them we were going to stop by for a visit. They were happy and excited that we were coming over.

As soon as Mama saw me, she said, "What's wrong? I can always tell when something isn't right with you. Sweetheart, what's wrong?" We all went into the kitchen because that's where we always met. Mama offered us something to eat or drink, and Frank told her, "No, thank you." Daddy stood off a bit, studying my demeanor. Frank was right by my side, holding my hand, and Daddy said, "What's wrong, baby girl? You know I can feel you." Him saying that made me burst into tears, which made Mama cry. They looked at each other, and Daddy said, "You found out, didn't you?" Through my tears, I said, "Are you my father?" Daddy said, "Of course, I am. Nothing will ever change that." He came over to me and held me, and I cried in his arms. Then I pushed away from him and said, "Why didn't you tell me? Why did you make me believe a lie? Does Cindy, Charles, or Amy know?" Mama said, "Baby, we're so sorry for not telling you. Your sisters and brother don't know either. As time went by, it got harder and harder, and there just never seemed to be a *right time*. Soon we never even thought about it because you were ours no matter what. We were all so happy, and we just didn't know what it would do to you or our family if we told you. Baby, please forgive us for not knowing how to handle it and hurting you." Daddy said, "Baby, we never, ever meant to hurt you. Please believe us." I told Frank, "I can't handle this right now. Take me home."

Mama tried to hug me, but I walked out. She cried in Daddy's arms. Frank told them to give me some time to digest things. "When she's ready, she'll reach out to you. Please be patient." It tore Frank up to see my family like this. He knew we've always been very close. He said to Daddy, "I know y'all are a praying family, so I believe that God will work all this out. Though we're not religious, Sabrina always tells me God will make a way. I have to believe that now."

Daddy shook Frank's hand and told him that he's a good man and to take good care of his baby girl.

I felt numb and took off on Monday. When I didn't show up for work, Rhonda called Frank to check on me. Of course, she called the day after I found out everything, but I didn't want to talk to anyone. She asked if she could come by after work to see me, and I told Frank yes. When she arrived, she hugged me tight and said she was there for me. We sat down, and she said, "Sabrina, I know you and Frank are good people and you don't go to church, so I'm not going to get religious on you. I just want you to know I've been praying for you guys since Saturday, and I feel like God wants me to tell you something." I looked at her with wide eyes because I was raised in a Christian home and understand these things. I just haven't decided that life was for me yet. I respect all Christians, but Frank and I are happy the way we are. However, I have the utmost respect for Christianity. My parents never pushed it on me. They always told me I had to decide for myself. I respected them so much for that.

Surprising Comfort

Rhonda shared some scriptures with us about the love of God, and I must admit, they were comforting. She encouraged me not to hold on to the anger or disappointment I was feeling toward my parents. "I'm sure your parents did what they thought was best at the time. Sabrina, they love you very much. Did they ever treat you any differently from your siblings?" I thought for a moment and said, "No. I couldn't tell at all. We were one big happy family. Daddy and Mama are great parents then and now." Rhonda told me to forgive them quickly so the devil doesn't have a foothold to try to dig things in deeper. I understood what she meant. Daddy used to tell us things like that while we were growing up. Frank was holding my hand and asked me, "Honey, are you okay? You know no matter what I'm here, right here with you." I smiled at him and squeezed his hand. Rhonda wrote down some scriptures and asked me to take some time and read them. She also told us that she was praying for us and that God loved us and promised never to leave us or forsake us. I saw Frank was in deep thought as she spoke. Then he asked, "So, Rhonda, are you saying God is really interested in us? In me?" "He sure is, Frank," Rhonda said. At this point, the room was quiet for a moment. We did a little more chitchat, and Rhonda said she was leaving. As we walked her to the door, she turned to me and said, "Sabrina, God loved you so much that he gave you a wonderful family to care for you and love you as their own. Girl, I'm telling you that's huge. I had so much respect for your parents before, but even more now. Some people were adopted into bad families. You're blessed, Sabrina!"

Both Frank and I took off that Tuesday. We sat down at the kitchen table and went over the scriptures Rhonda gave us. The room seemed as if it were filled with something I just couldn't explain. Frank said he felt it too. It was warmth, love, and joy all together; at least that's how it seemed to me. Frank and I decided we should start going to church and we were going to talk some more with Rhonda. I told Frank I wanted to go to my parents' house and talk to them, and he made it happen. Mama told Frank to come for lunch. When we got there, not only were Mama and Daddy there, but also Cindy, Charles, and Amy. Amy grabbed me and hugged me, followed by Charles and Cindy. Charles said,

"Sabrina, you're our sister. No piece of paper can change that. Mama and Daddy did what they thought was the right thing to do at the time." I stopped him and said, "I know they did." Mama cried tears of joy as she shook her head up and down. I said, "Frank and I talked about it, and we prayed with Rhonda." When I said that, Daddy looked up with happiness in his eyes. I continued, "I haven't told Frank this yet, but I don't want to know about my biological father." Frank said, "Are you sure, baby?" "Yeah, I've thought about it a lot. I know he wants to meet me, but what would meeting me do?" Then Daddy said, "Well, maybe it's something that he needs to do. As a father, I can't imagine how he must feel, but the fact that he wants to meet you says it's been on his mind and who knows for how long. But, baby girl, it's your call." We had a wonderful visit with the family, and they all told me they were 100 percent supportive of whatever I decided to do. Frank was with me all the way; he never left my side.

The next day, we went to work. Kathy came over to me and hugged me and said she was in my corner. I told her all was well and we were moving forward. Then Ralph and Bert joined us, and I told them that I had decided I wasn't going to meet my real father but that I thought I would now with my family's blessing and support. They told me I had theirs too.

Truth Revealed

So Frank and I decided to meet him. Arrangements were made, and we met for lunch. Frank and I were sitting at the table, waiting for him to arrive. He looked at me and told me how proud he was of me. Just then, he looked over toward the door and said, "Oh my god, that's got to be him." There he was looking like a male version of me. All I could say was, "Wow!" The waitress brought him over to our table. He looked a bit nervous and said, "Sabrina?" I said, "Yes." He handed me a bouquet of beautiful roses and shook Frank's hand. "I'm Myles Holloway. It's a pleasure meeting you both." Frank was standing along with Mr. Holloway. I was seated but slowly stood up, staring at him the whole time. I didn't feel anger, hate, or anything bad. Actually, I felt happy to meet him. I was so surprised. He extended his hand to me, and I shook it while still staring at him. Suddenly, I said, "I look like you." He said, "You sure do. Wow!" We all sat down. Mr. Holloway said, "I'm sorry if I've caused you any pain. I didn't know about you until recently. Can I explain?" "Yes, please do!" I said. "Your birth mother recently passed away, and on her deathbed, she told me about you. We remained friends over the years, but not close friends. She never told me about you. She got sick and knew she was dying and asked my sister to have me come see her. She gave me this package and asked me to give it to you. As soon as I found out about you, I wanted to meet you. I don't want to interrupt your life or cause trouble for you. I just wanted to meet my daughter. You see, I have no other children." In the package were pictures of me at birth through the time of adoption; my mother, who was gorgeous; and letters she wrote me over the years. Mr. Holloway told me she was very poor growing up and she was young and couldn't afford to care for me. She said it was very hard, but to give me a good life, she made the hardest decision she ever made in her life. As I read her letters, I could feel her pain with that decision but the hope of a great life for me. Mr. Holloway was a very classy dresser and smelled good. I could tell he had very good taste. I guess that's where I got my flare for fashion from. We enjoyed a very lovely visit and decided to remain in each other's lives. By the time we finished lunch, we weren't calling him Mr. Holloway anymore; we were calling him Myles. We even found out he was a Christian.

Eventually, Myles met my family, and we all got along well. Frank surprised me one Friday night after I got home late from work by telling me Myles led him to the Lord. "I'm a Christian now, Sabrina, and want you to join me. Will you?" I laughed and told him Rhonda led me and Bert to the Lord this evening, which was part of the reason I was late. We laughed and called Mama and Daddy to tell them. They were so excited. That was all Rhonda and Bert needed; they were now a couple.

That night, as we lay in bed, I had my head on Frank's chest. I told him, "I remember when all this started with the private investigator taking pictures and how you took charge right from the start. Frank, I saw you take action and protect me. I noticed it but, with all that was going on, failed to mention it to you. But now I want you to know, through this whole thing, you made me feel so safe and secure. I love you so much, Frank!" Frank kissed me on the forehead and said, "I'll always protect you, Sabrina. You're my wife, my good thing!" I blushed and told him I was falling in love with him all over again and again and again . . . You get the message.

To add to the excitement, I found out I was four months pregnant and ended up having twins, a girl and a boy. So Myles went from having no children to having a daughter, a son-in-law, and two grandchildren. God has been so good to us. From time to time, I think about my birth mother. I put the picture she gave me of herself holding me as a newborn in a frame. I've met her family and Myles's family too. Daddy and Mama taught me that the heart is ever expanding with love. I also found out that I don't mind my husband being passive anymore because when he needs to be a lion and protect me and our children, he roars loudly!

CPSIA information can be obtained
at www.ICGtesting.com
Printed in the USA
LVHW100109060623
748929LV00002B/460